Y STORIES

For younger readers

DRAGON RIDE
TEVER HAPPENED AT WINKLESEA

books for
books for child
of which have bee
antiques (she hopes eventual
painting, walking in the country

WHA

STONESTRUCK

Helen Cresswell

PUFFIN BOOKS

For Colin, with love

PUFFIN BOOKS

Published by the Penguin Group
Penguin Books Ltd, 27 Wrights Lane, London W8 5TZ, England
Penguin Books USA Inc., 375 Hudson Street, New York, New York 10014, USA
Penguin Books Australia Ltd, Ringwood, Victoria, Australia
Penguin Books Canada Ltd, 10 Alcorn Avenue, Toronto, Ontario, Canada M4V 3B2
Penguin Books (NZ) Ltd, 182–190 Wairau Road, Auckland 10, New Zealand

Penguin Books Ltd, Registered Offices: Harmondsworth, Middlesex, England

First published by Viking 1995
Published in Puffin Books 1996
9

Filmset in Baskerville

Made and printed in Great Britain by Clays Ltd, St Ives plc

Prologue

J essica ... Jessica ... a whispering sort
name that seems to dissolve on your tongue even as
you say it.

Mist ... a whispering sort of word, and whispering
weather, too. Mist muffles footfall, blots up birdsong
and through it the trees, people, houses are seen as only
whispers of their real selves. Mountains, of course, disappear altogether.

The Welsh border, where Wales and England meet,
is haunted country. There are misty hills and secret
valleys, dark ridges whose slopes are trodden only by
sheep and their lonely shepherds. In this landscape
there have been whispered stories of strange happenings,
of wizards and spells, of changelings, disappearances.
Some of these stories have been written down and some
have not.

Welshpool is full of stories that have never been
written down – till now. They have been passed on by
whisper, from generation to generation. Even today the
people of Welshpool do not tell such stories aloud, and
they never tell them to strangers. They have heard of
strangers who come and go, appear and vanish – like
mist itself.

And the word they whisper most of all is 'castle'. Welshpool is a small town that sprawls on a hillside. Half-way up that hill you can turn off along a side lane that leads to great wrought-iron gates. Beyond, through the innocent-seeming meadows with the pools and shining buttercups, runs the back way to a castle – Powis Castle. And it is there that the magic gathers. It gathers, coils itself up like a spring and is released – in mist.

When mist falls the people of Welshpool hurry to their homes and shut the doors, but only when they have called their children in. The children, playing in the streets as their shadows fly like shuttles under the lamplight, hear their names called and scatter. They run for home and safety, and yelp as they spy other running shapes in the mist – shapes that they may, or may not, know.

Because it is children who vanish in Welshpool, children who come and go. There are tales of games of hide-and-seek when the seeker vanished, never to be seen again. There are stories of chains of rough children, hands linked, running through the town, hobnailed boots clattering.

In places like Welshpool superstitions breed and grow. And the one that every single man, woman and child believes, the one that strikes a chill whenever it is spoken, is, 'Never count children twice. Ever.'

One

'Jessica! Jessica!'

Her nightmare was shattered, there was an instant of waking and then the other nightmare was there – the real one.

'Quickly! Here's your coat!'

Jessica blinked in the torchlight and thrust her arms into the sleeves. She automatically sat and pulled on her thick woollen stockings, then her shoes. The long, eerie wail of the siren was dying now, and out in the dark streets she could hear running footsteps, shouts. Soon there would be the steady drone of aeroplanes, and after that the whine of shells, the thuds.

'Hurry!'

'I *am*!'

'Got your gas mask?'

Jessica snatched it up from her bedside, and with it the book she was reading.

'Henry!'

'Oh, *leave* him – he never stays down there anyway.'

'Oh, Mum! Shine the torch!'

The beam swung about the room and Jessica saw him, curled on the chair. He uttered his usual protest as she scooped him up, warm and slack with sleep.

She followed her mother, only a shape and a shadow, and the rocking beam of the torch down the stairs and then down the narrow stone steps of the cellar. The smell came up to meet her, fusty, dank, cold. Already Jessica was shivering. She felt sick.

'When the war's over I'll never come down to the cellar again,' she told herself. 'Ever.'

There was the paraffin smell as her mother lit the lamp and stove. For hours now the pair of them would be imprisoned down there in that stone cell.

She let Henry slip from her grasp and he set off, stalking the cellar as he always did. He would not stay. He would sniff the icy corners, dab the odd spider, then wend his lordly way back up the stone steps to the warm, dangerous house. Jessica had given up trying to stop him.

She sat on the edge of her bunk-bed.

'Ugh! It smells like a tomb!'

'I should lie down, while you're still warm, and try to get back to sleep.'

'I'm not warm, I'm frozen. And if the house gets hit and collapses it'll *be* a tomb. We'll be trapped. They might never find us.'

Even as she spoke Jessica's eyes were roving about for spiders. She knew they were harmless, but nevertheless they were a small nightmare within the big one. She saw that Henry, tail high, was already padding towards the steps.

'Oh, Henry!' she sighed, and watched him go.

As he melted into the gloom there was a series of muffled thuds. The raid had begun.

'That sounded close,' she said, and shivered.

Her mother was sitting now, and had taken out her

4

knitting. Beside her on the table were the flask of tea she always brought down, the gas masks, the box with the glucose tablets and barley sugar and the biscuit tin. In the shadows beyond, Jessica saw something new. A suitcase.

'What's in there – that case?'

Her mother began knitting, did not look up.

'I'll tell you later. A surprise.'

'Oh, Mum! Now I'll never get to sleep.'

'You will.'

'It's funny,' Jessica said. 'Part of me wants to go to sleep, to get away from everything. I hate it down here.'

'We're lucky to have a cellar. At least we don't have to go traipsing to the Underground.'

'And part of me wants to stay awake, because I'm scared that if I go to sleep something terrible will happen. It's as if when I'm awake I can stop it happening.'

'Funny girl.'

'I'm a terrible coward, aren't I?'

'Everyone's frightened. I don't suppose you're any more frightened than anyone else.'

'I bet I am. I bet I'm the biggest coward in the whole world. I – ooooh!'

She screamed.

Her very bones jarred, the stones of the cellar seemed to rock. Jessica's hands flew to her ears and her eyes squeezed tight shut as if cutting out sound and sight could cancel out the horror, make it go away.

'Mum! Mum!'

She felt arms about her and buried herself into the rough tweed and as she did so had a swift memory of burying herself into the thick khaki of her father's coat and crying, 'Dad! Dad! Don't go!'

She was fighting for air now and pulled herself away, and at once started to choke, and heard her mother gasping too. Jessica opened her eyes and saw only a thick, drifting pall of dust. She could just make out a faint disc where the lamp was, like sun through mist. Her hands dropped from her ears. She heard rattles, the creak of timber, a distant banging as if of wind blowing a door to and fro. Already the dust was stinging her eyes and she rubbed at them furiously.

'Mum! Oh, Mum!'

She heard her own wail float thinly in the dust as if it came from someone else.

The cloud was beginning to settle; they could breathe again, and see. The silence was enormous. They looked at one another, faces blackened and stunned.

'It's my nightmare,' Jessica heard herself whisper. 'It's my nightmare come true. We're buried, aren't we?'

'Stay there.'

Her mother got to her feet and stood for a moment unsteadily, straining through the dust for the stone steps. She began to move towards them.

'Mum! Don't go!'

Jessica clutched at her coat.

'Stay there!' She was pushed down again and fell sideways on the bunk.

'Oh, please . . . please . . .' she whispered. What she meant was, 'Please make it not have happened, please let it only be a dream, please make the world go away!'

She actually managed to go into a kind of silence and darkness where the world did not exist and where she herself had disappeared. She did not know how long

6

she stayed in that limbo. She wanted to stay for ever. Then the bed lurched as her mother sat heavily beside her. A hand was stroking her hair.

'Just lie there, darling. They'll soon get us out.'

The words came spinning into the darkness inside Jessica's head. They hovered there while she groped for their meaning. Then she understood. She sat up.

'We *are* trapped!'

'Something must have fallen against the door. It won't open.'

'But we didn't shut it! We never do!'

Her mother left the cellar door ajar. Jessica was always comforted by the knowledge. It made the cellar less of a dungeon, a tomb.

'Something must have fallen against it.'

'We're trapped. We're trapped!'

'Jessica! Stop it!'

'Why won't you *admit* it? You're always trying to pretend things aren't bad when they are!'

As soon as the words were out she was appalled by them. She had not meant to say them, even though they were true. There was a long silence – or part silence. Thud. Thud thud thud. Further away now. She stole a sideways look at her mother.

'I'm going to have to put the stove out. And the light.'

'Oh no!'

'They give off fumes. The door's tight shut.'

Jessica gave up. Things could not be any worse now.

'Henry . . .' she whispered, remembering. 'He's up there. Oh, Henry . . .'

And then the light went out and there was total darkness.

*

Jessica never knew how long that darkness lasted. She remembered so little about it that she was not really sure whether she had been awake or asleep. She had seemed to occupy a kind of no man's land, suspended in time and space.

She never saw the burning houses in the square, the sky criss-crossed with the sweeping spokes of searchlights. She did not hear the shouts and screams or even, just as dawn was breaking, the high monotonous wail of the all-clear. She and her mother did talk a little, she remembered that.

'Will – will the house be still there?'

'I don't know. Oh, if only –'

'If only what?'

'Nothing. If only you'd been already in Wales!'

'But term doesn't start for ages yet. I don't want to go to Wales, anyway.'

'The whole school's going.'

'But *you're* not.'

'And to a castle! I should've loved to have gone to school in a castle.'

'Well, I don't.'

'At least you'll be safe.'

'I shan't. I'll never be safe . . .'

They had had this conversation before. They had had it regularly, ever since it was announced that Jessica's school was to be evacuated to Wales.

'And not just any old where,' the headmistress had told them in assembly. 'A castle in Wales – Powis Castle!'

A stir ran through the rows of girls, sitting cross-legged and goody-goody in their green and gold uniforms.

'We shall travel there by train, the day before the next term starts. Your parents have already been informed. And the school will remain there until it is safe to return to London.'

She had gone on to make a feeble joke about how safe it would be – 'No bombs there – perhaps just a few flying arrows!' – and some pupils had tittered obligingly. Some of them were excited. Jessica, right from the start, had felt only dread. Her father had left six months ago, already a stranger in his khaki uniform, for some mysterious place called 'the Front'.

It was made more mysterious by the fact that it was never given a proper name. No one seemed to know where it was. It was just 'the Front'. Jessica and her mother went to the cinema, and always before the main film there were newsreels. They showed women in turbans working in munitions factories, men in allotments digging for victory. They showed aeroplanes, tanks and battleships, and marching columns of men. Jessica would strain up at the flickering black-and-white pictures, but those marching men were always going *to* the Front, were never actually there. The man who read the news sounded cheerful and excited, and talked a lot about 'the enemy'. But just as Jessica never once caught a glimpse of her father among those marching soldiers, so she never saw the face of the enemy.

She knew that despite the cheerfulness of the newsreels, people who went to the Front did not always come back. They went missing. She felt that if only she could have kept her father in sight, he would be safe, could not possibly go missing. Nothing could happen to him if she were there. But he had gone, on a long, crowded train, with hundreds of other men all in the same khaki.

9

The cold religious light had come shafting down from the vaulted station roof as if in a cathedral. It lit eerily the thronged platforms and pale faces of forlorn families huddled in groups. Jessica had never seen so many people weeping as on that day. She had certainly never before seen men crying.

Now she was to go to Wales and leave her mother in London − out of sight. Who then would be there to protect her on nights when the sky rained fire . . .?

The long cold darkness in the cellar came to an end around dawn.

'Listen!' Jessica caught her mother's arm.

There were voices, bangs, clattering. Her mother switched on the torch, ran up the steps and was hammering on the door.

'Here! We're here! Help!'

Jessica groped her way after her.

'Help! Help!' she screamed, with all the pent-up terror of the night.

'Coming! Hold on!' The voice was comfortingly close, only the other side of the door. Soon there were other voices and the sounds of rubble being cleared.

'There we go!'

Next minute the door was open and the pair were blinking in the sudden light.

'You all right, Mrs Weaver? Here we are, young Jess − *here* we go!'

She found herself being lifted, had a swift glimpse of the littered space that had been the hall, and was set down in the road. She rocked, and a hand steadied her.

'Anyone else in there, Mrs Weaver?'

Jessica was aware that the road, the pavement, was

strewn with rubble. There was an acrid smell of burning. Slowly she raised her eyes.

She saw what she had dreaded, what she had seen many times in her mind's eye during that endless wait. But what she saw now was in an eerie and unimagined detail. She stared at the blue curtains of her own room, blowing out in rags. Her bed, chair, dressing-table tilted on a floor that had half slipped into the room below. She saw the cabbage roses of the wallpaper in the living-room, the jumble of books, cushions, pictures. The cast-iron bath was improbably balanced in the debris like a huge white pig.

She looked down. A toothbrush lay by her feet. She stooped mechanically and picked it up. It was yellow. Hers. She had used it last night, diligently brushing her teeth up and down, side to side.

It suddenly struck her as impossibly funny, that shipwrecked and salvaged toothbrush. She heard herself starting to laugh in a high-pitched, jerky way.

'Jessica! Stop it!' Her mother was shaking her.

'My – toothbrush!' Jessica spluttered, and held it out.

'Come along now. We'll have a nice hot cup of tea.'

Jessica, still clutching her toothbrush, allowed herself to be towed along. They picked their way through the rubble to the end of the square.

'Here, please,' she heard her mother say, and was aware then that an ARP warden was with them, carrying the suitcase from the cellar. He put it down, and went.

'Oh, you poor things! Come in, come in!'

It was Mrs Latimer, a friend of her mother's whose own two sons were away at the Front. Numbly Jessica sat, accepted a cup of tea and a biscuit. There was no glass left in the windows, and the room felt curiously light and out of doors, not a real room at all.

'Something must have told me to take it down there,' her mother was saying. 'She'd have had to go off without anything, otherwise.'

'What a shame for her to have to go off like this, though,' Mrs Latimer said. 'She must be terribly shocked.'

'I – I haven't told her yet.' Her mother's voice was lowered now. Immediately Jessica pricked up her ears. When grown-ups lowered their voices it was always worth listening. 'I thought it better for her not – not to be brooding about it.'

'And when do you go?'

'Friday.'

Jessica lifted her head.

'When do you go where?' she asked, very distinctly.

She saw the swiftly exchanged glances, heard the 'Oh dear!' from Mrs Latimer.

'Jessica . . . I didn't tell you before . . . I didn't want you to worry.'

'Tell me what?'

'I'm – going to Belgium. To drive ambulances. And . . . I've arranged for you to go to Powis now – before term starts.'

'When?' This was not happening. It couldn't be.

'This afternoon. Half-past three.' Gently, 'I'm sorry. If only –'

'No!' Jessica was on her feet, spilling tea. Then, 'Henry! Where is he?'

She ran then, out of the room, out of the house, back into the smoking, blackened square.

'Henry! Henry!'

She reached her house, the jagged gap where the front door had been.

'No, missy, you can't go in there! Whole thing could cave in at any minute! Where's your –'

She shook herself free and raced on, jumping over blackened beams, dodging great clumps of bricks and mortar. She ran because she was trying to disappear. She knew, of course, that she could not actually disappear, but ran as if by running hard and long enough she would come as near to it as a human being possibly can. She ran because she couldn't think of anything else to do.

When she finally stopped, heaving for breath, she was in a street that was still burning fiercely. Other people's curtains, beds, books, clothes were being devoured by flames. A few yards away was a pile of rubble still smouldering. Beyond it, veiled by smoke, she saw a boy standing. Her eyes met his.

About them men were running with hoses, ladders, stretchers. They alone stood motionless. The boy was looking at Jessica and she at him as if they were the last two people left alive in the world. His eyes in his grimed face were so pale they seemed silver. He seemed in another world, wreathed in smoke and framed by fire.

It was a strange meeting, wordless, because there were no words to say. Jessica knew that it must be his home that was burning behind him.

'Jessica!' She heard her name called, far away as if in a dream. She did not even turn her head.

The station was thronged with men in khaki. Jessica's head ached with the noise. Her mother found a seat by the window, and a young soldier swung her case up on to the rack. She stood by the open window, looking at her mother.

'Why?' she asked again out of her misery. 'Why?'

'I must go. Everyone's got to do their bit. Daddy's doing his. There's a war on.' Her mother's voice was barely more than a whisper. She did not want people to hear, didn't want any feelings on show.

'I *know* there's a war!' Jessica hissed. 'But what about me, what about *me*?'

Her mother seemed a stranger now, seemed to have gone away already.

'You don't care!' said Jessica bitterly.

'You must try to be brave. We all must.'

'I'm not brave. I don't feel brave.'

'Come on now, love. Give me a smile.'

Jessica gazed mutely and coldly back at her mother. Doors were slamming, guards shouting.

'Oh – you're off! Oh, Jessica!'

She reached up and they embraced awkwardly. The whistle blew and the train hissed.

'Goodbye! Goodbye!'

The train drew off and her mother kept pace with it, waving and calling. Jessica saw the tears running down her cheeks and then a cloud of steam drifted past the window. When it cleared, she had gone.

Two

It was late evening and already dusk when the train drew into Welshpool. By then the carriage had emptied. The noisy, card-playing soldiers had gone spilling off, station by station, to be met by mothers, wives, children.

Jessica sat alone and gazed out at the wide, darkening sky and the hills.

'The world's gone empty,' she thought.

She had never before been alone and travelling to an unknown destination to live among strangers. She had never even dreamed of it. She watched as the hills, littered with sheep, became mountains. They rose steeply on either side, shutting out the sky.

Jessica felt herself a traveller in a foreign land.

The steady clackety-clack of the wheels changed to a different rhythm. The train was slowing. She felt for her suitcase, just by her knees where the soldier had put it, saying, 'Don't you forget it, now. Cheer up, girlie!'

She got stiffly to her feet and tugged at the leather window strap. She had just managed to free it as the train drew to a halt, brakes grinding.

'Welshpool! This is Welshpool!'

She climbed down on to the platform and tugged the

case after her. She looked about. Was this a station? No vaulted roof, no throngs of people. The steam blew past her in ribbons.

'Jessica? Jessica, is it?'

The woman was quite old, grey hair pushed under her felt hat, and hardly taller than Jessica herself. She nodded.

'Ah – and such a journey you've had! Come along now with me, and we'll soon have you to rights! Mrs Lockett, I am!' – this last over her shoulder.

Jessica followed. When they reached a wicket gate Mrs Lockett stopped and began to babble in a high voice to two men in peaked caps. They all looked at Jessica, still talking, and she could not understand a word they were saying, and realized with a shock that they were speaking Welsh.

'So you're the first from London, then?' The man was smiling. They were all smiling. 'There'll be plenty more to come, so they say.'

'This is Lockett – give him your case, dear,' said Mrs Lockett, 'and he'll put it in the car.'

The shorter of the two men took the case and they followed him out to the station yard.

'Not really the chauffeur,' Mrs Lockett confided. 'Head gardener, filling in. Real chauffeur's gone to the Front.'

The car drew off. They drove first between mountains, then quite soon were dropping into Welshpool itself. Jessica gazed numbly through the glass at the deserted, darkening streets and blind grey houses. Halfway down the hill they turned right.

'Going the back way,' said Mrs Lockett. 'The castle – see!'

She pointed. Jessica saw the great bulk of the castle against the streaked sky. It stood on a high mound, and around spread wooded parkland. It looked massive, mysterious. It did not, in a million years, look like home.

Then she saw the deer. They came gliding out into this cold dewfall, quietly assembling from their daytime hiding places. They bowed their slender necks and grazed the turf. To Jessica they seemed remote as unicorns, marvellously peaceful and innocent. Their movements were patterned and ceremonious, as if they wove a long-established dance through a twilight centuries old. She was entranced.

As the car drove up the steep road to the castle she turned her head to keep them in sight. Then they were cut off by a stone wall. The car passed under a wide stone arch into a courtyard, and drew up.

'Here we are, then!' Mrs Lockett was already out. Jessica followed. The air was suddenly icy cold and she stood swaying, dizzy.

'All right, are you?'

The voice sounded far away. In the half darkness there came a harsh scream. It tore the peaceful air, echoed in the stone courtyard.

Jessica shivered. Again that piercing scream. It came out of a vast emptiness. It was as if it struck against the very roof of the world. The silence when it faded was enormous.

She closed her eyes. Then Mrs Lockett was there.

'Come along now, dear – bed, isn't it?'

Jessica followed in a trance. It was as if she had been torn apart by that high-pitched scream, and some part of her was now running free, separate. She followed

Mrs Lockett into the different cold of the castle, and was absolutely aware that part of her was still out there, in the gathering darkness.

When she woke Jessica saw bare white walls flooded gold, and heard a deafening chorus of birdsong. She lay waiting for familiar sounds in the street, and remembered that she was in Wales, in a castle. Then she remembered the bomb, the long darkness in the cellar, her bedroom curtains flying in tatters. She remembered that she did not know where either her father or mother were. A wave of blackness washed over her, of panic, as if she were balanced above a sheer drop.

She was out of bed and pulling on her things, and then out of the room, hoping to leave the dread behind her. The passageway was stone and cold; it smelled of the cellar at home. She hurried along it searching for a way out, a way into the open. Then she could smell fresh air and saw a door, ajar. She pulled thankfully at the heavy metal ring and next moment was out in the courtyard.

On the opposite side she saw a stone arch and another door, or gate, also half open. She made for it like an escaping prisoner. Once through she drew a deep breath and looked about her.

To her right she saw the deer, still calmly grazing as if they had been cropping there all night long in the moonlight. Even in the thin washed gold of dawn they were magical and separate, moving in their own dimension. The great trees of the park threw long shadows, telling the time.

She stood and gazed and wished herself a deer. There

was a scream, that same high scream she had heard the night before. She stood frozen, transfixed.

Turning, she saw, unimagined and impossible, a peacock. He gleamed green and gold and blue, amazing. He pivoted, and out came his skirt, his brilliant painted fan. It was a private show, meant only for her. She could hear the swish of the unfurling, and the tiny scuffing of peacock steps on stone. He blazed and shone and wheeled and was a miracle.

Then he tilted his crested head and uttered a high, raucous screech and in the instant Jessica understood, and found herself laughing with relief.

'It was *you*!'

The peacock considered her for a moment then turned and walked lordly away down the path, and she followed. The great fan dipped and swayed.

They passed through a wicket gate and were on a wide terrace. To her right Jessica glimpsed the shine of water, but the peacock turned left, and she was following her leader. She followed in a kind of dream, and hardly saw the flowers, the statues, the ancient yews.

The peacock stopped. Slowly, shudderingly, the amazing fan collapsed and fell.

'Aaaah!' She felt a sudden chill, and shivered.

Lifting her eyes from the ruined fan she saw ahead a band of thick white mist.

'But . . .?' She glanced behind, where the morning was clear and yellow.

'Jessica . . . Jessica . . . Jessica . . .'

The whispers were coming from that swirl of mist.

'Jessica . . . Jessica . . . Jessica . . .'

The voices were soft, coaxing, an invitation. She thought she heard laughter, too, children's laughter.

She took a step forward. But a part of her mind that was still working told her that mist never comes in patches as dense as this on a clear day. It told her that it was dawn, too early for children to be playing. It told her, too, that whoever these children were, they could not possibly know her name.

'Jessica . . . Jessica . . .'

And yet whoever it was did know her name, and so had a secret and strong power over her. As she stood staring into the whiteness, she glimpsed a shape, thought she saw a hand beckon.

She screamed then.

'No!'

She fled back along the terrace, feet and heart thudding, skin flashing with terror. She did not stop until she was out of the gardens, back through the wicket gate where the peacock had led her.

The peacock! She turned and looked behind. He was not there.

'Flown off,' she thought. 'Must have.'

The deer were still there. That, for some curious reason, was a relief.

'Should've thought you'd have slept till eleven,' said Mrs Lockett at breakfast. 'White as a ghost and fit to drop.'

'I do sometimes, at home.'

'Do you?'

'When we've been in the cellar. When there's a raid.'

'Oooh, terrible, that must be. I can hardly imagine . . .'

She paused, but Jessica did not feel like filling in the gap. She did not want to talk about cellars and raids.

'And for such a thing to happen to your own home,' went on Mrs Lockett. 'Terrible.' She sighed. 'What'll you do with yourself?'

'Do?'

'Till your school comes. What'll you do? Not used to children, see, having none of my own.'

'I'll be all right.'

'Mustn't get too near that pool down the wilderness, mind. That much I do know. Children and water don't mix.'

'I won't. I saw the peacock this morning. I hadn't realized. When I heard that scream last night, I couldn't –'

She broke off, seeing Mrs Lockett's face.

'Scream?'

'Yes. When we got here, remember.'

'I heard no scream.'

It was Jessica's turn to stare.

'You must have!'

'No!' Mrs Lockett's voice was barely a whisper. There was a long silence.

'And you saw – a *peacock*?'

'Yes. This morning. And then I realized that the scream –'

'There are no peacocks,' said Mrs Lockett.

'But –' Jessica was dazed. That bird with its brilliant spread of feathers – she could not have imagined it, surely?

'There've been no peacocks here for years and years. They're ill luck. The family won't have them.'

Slowly Jessica shook her head. She felt strangely light-headed, as if the world were slipping away from her.

'Whatever could have made you imagine such a thing?'

Jessica looked at Mrs Lockett and saw that her face was flushed and angry – or was it frightened? Again she shook her head.

'I don't know.'

'You heard no scream and you saw no peacock. Imagining things. Must've been the shock.'

Jessica bowed her head.

'Yes. Shock, see. Does funny things.'

Still Jessica stared at her plate, seeing that blazing bird. The telephone rang.

'Oh, you is it, Megan . . . oh yes . . . oh, there never! *How* many? Seven o'clock train . . .?'

At last she put the receiver down.

'Evacuees,' she said. 'Over thirty, she says!'

Jessica looked at her, saying nothing.

'That's what I am,' she thought. 'An evacuee . . .'

Mrs Lockett went straight off to Welshpool after breakfast. There was no end to be done, she assured Jessica. Beds organized, homes found, food arranged. Jessica could stay behind and explore the castle and grounds.

'And keep away from the water, mind!'

Mrs Lockett went scuttling off over the meadows to Welshpool. The deer had vanished, gone to their secret daytime haunts. One day, Jessica told herself, she would go searching for them in those woods and spinneys. But not today.

When she reached the wicket gate that led to the gardens she stepped through it a different person entirely from the one who had followed that bright peacock. As she walked slowly along the broad terrace it was as if she were doing so for the first time.

'Because I didn't see anything, except the peacock,' she told herself. 'I didn't see those statues up there, or even the castle. Perhaps I *was* in a kind of dream.'

She looked up at the castle now and was amazed by its colour. It was not at all the serious grey you would expect. Rounded towers, battlements, turrets were all of stone, but of a deep, rosy pink. They looked as if they were bathed in the light of a perpetually setting sun.

'More like an enchanted castle,' she thought. 'One out of a fairy-tale, like the Sleeping Beauty's. One under a spell.'

What struck her most of all was the yews. They crouched on the steep hillside, straddled the terraces, like great leathery beasts, dinosaurs. They were folded and tucked and full of crevices, so ancient that they seemed to have a power of their own, a power drawn up over the centuries. Jessica was awestruck by them, as she was in cathedrals.

'Old as cathedrals these are. Easily.'

She turned to look over the valley, and the spring trees were ablaze like green bonfires, and she thought that she had never seen such green before.

'It's green gone mad!' And she felt a stir of excitement, as though something in herself, too, were greening over.

She reached the end of the walk and saw a flight of stone steps leading up. She climbed them, and was on another terrace, and built into the hillside was an orangery. She peered in. It was all white and green, and she saw the stern stone heads of men, wreathed in foliage.

She climbed the next flight of steps and found herself on yet another terrace. On the balustrade were statues, some piping, some dancing, their leaden skirts flying in the windless air.

There was a long recess built into the hillside, with seven mellowed brick arches. Jessica walked through one, treading the shattered pink floor. The walls were decorated with ferns and ivies, and honeysuckle tumbled from the arched roof. She wound absently along, in one arch and out of the next, and as she did so a faint gleam caught her eye. She bent to the foot of an ivy, and saw a small blue bowl, and in it biscuits and an apple.

'Jessica . . . Jessica . . . Jessica . . .'

She leapt as if stung and looked swiftly about her. The children! Those same children, surely, who had been there in the mist that morning. She waited, intent, and half listening for the cry of a peacock. She heard nothing — or almost nothing. Someone had once told her that out of doors there was no such thing as absolute silence.

'Cuckoo! Cuckoo!'

It was as if her thoughts had been read. She looked down again at the half-concealed bowl, and shook her head.

'Funny . . .'

She retraced her steps, then followed a steep path that led downward, and found herself actually inside one of the great yews. She had to pass through it because it formed a tunnel that widened into a kind of tree cave. She stood sniffing its dry, ancient smell and staring up at its wizened centre. It covered and enfolded her.

'You could almost live in here,' she thought.

No rain could penetrate those thick walls of yew. Even in winter the snow would scarcely drift into the dry heart of it. You could lie low there, like a fox, make a bed of leaves and be snug and secret. She reached up and fingered the dry wood, and as she did so something caught her eye. It was a drawstring bag, of hessian or sacking, hanging from a short branch. She reached and unhooked the string, then pulled the bag open. There were apples and a loaf.

Whatever . . .?

Was someone, perhaps, living in the yew hedge, and was this their larder? And what of the bowl hidden by the foot of the ivy under the stone arches? Perhaps the food had been left there by a gardener, she told herself. But she did not believe it. She drew the strings again and hooked the bag on its branch. Still wondering, she passed through the yew and on to the steep path downwards, where all was open, neat and orderly, with no possibility of whispers or imaginary peacocks.

The garden she found herself in was formal, symmetrical, laid out in a pattern. She wandered along the straight paths and was soothed by the sheer predictability of it all. Everything was matching and neat. It was a garden good as gold, trained to behave itself. There were knobbed and silvery apple trees obediently stretching out their arms, held by strings and crusted with lichen like grey coral. At their feet were matching, spiky clumps of green and silver leaves, like shoes. Beyond she could see a fountain, and even a fountain is water doing what it is told to do.

'Morning!'

She jumped. It was an old man, sitting on a bench and eating.

'Having a look round, are you?'

She nodded.

'Don't recognize me, do you? Not without the cap.'

'Oh – Mr Lockett!'

'Lockett. *Mr* Lockett in the town – or George, depending – and Lockett here at the castle. Funny, that . . .'

He chewed ruminatively.

'Always bring my breakfast out, except in the winter. Live out of doors if I could, Mrs Lockett says.'

Jessica smiled.

'You're a very good gardener.'

'Like my grandfather. And like *his* father, too.'

'So he's always lived at the castle,' Jessica thought. 'He'll know about peacocks and whispering voices.'

'Mr Lockett . . .'

'Lockett.'

'Lockett . . . have there ever been peacocks at the castle?'

He looked at her then.

'The family won't have peacocks. They're ill luck.'

There was a pause.

'But you heard one?'

She nodded.

'Already . . .' He sighed. 'You're unhappy . . .'

She nodded again.

'Listen,' he said, 'you're unhappy now, but one day you will be happy.'

She was bewildered. What was he telling her?

'They say that when a peacock screams, it's a sign of rain coming,' he said. 'Here, at Powis, it's a sign of tears . . .'

'But why? Why?'

'There's a story . . .'

She waited.

'I sometimes think it gathers power with the telling,' he said, as if to himself.

'Tell me. Please.'

He looked at her, then shook his head.

'Not now. Later, maybe. But mind you one thing.'

She waited.

'You mind what you wish. That's all. Mind what you wish.'

Three

'Only the first, this lot,' Mrs Lockett said at teatime. 'More to come, they say.'

Jessica said nothing.

'It'll be nice for you, Jessica. Other London children.'

'Yes.' She did not mean it. Did Mrs Lockett think that all the children in London knew one another? Or did she mean that they were different from children anywhere else – Welshpool, say?

'Come with me, if you like, to meet the train. Like that, would you?'

'Is it a school that's coming?'

'Bless you no! From all over everywhere, from what I gather. Brothers and sisters, some of them, though whether they'll be kept together ... poor mites ... Anyway, for their own good.'

'Not good, exactly.' It was Lockett, who hardly ever spoke. Perhaps the long hours he spent alone in the castle gardens made speech grow rusty. Or perhaps he only spoke when there was something worth saying.

'Good? Of course it's good!' His wife was indignant. 'All those bombs – and here as quiet and safe –'

'Not good their being fetched from their families I

mean, Rhoda,' he said. 'Meant to be with their mams and dads, children are. Jessica here – she'd rather – wouldn't you?'

'I'd rather have stayed with Mum,' she said. 'It's nice here, and I know it's safer from bombs, but . . .'

She did not know how to say it. She did not know how to say that in coming to Powis, in not even knowing where her parents were, she had lost the only real safety she knew. That the world had at a stroke become wide and dangerous. That she herself felt curiously that she was no longer herself, was cut adrift, floating in time and space.

'Anyway, come with me if you like, to meet the train. You'll like that.'

And so at half-past six they left the castle, Mrs Lockett with her trays of scones and tarts, Lockett wearing his chauffeur's cap, sitting oddly above his gardening shirt and corduroys.

This time as they drove through Welshpool it was alive and spilling on to the streets in the mild April evening. Men stood in groups, children ran and chased and played hopscotch and the streets were lit with a golden theatrical light. The stage was set for the entrance of the children from London, the strangers, the evacuees.

At the station the waiting-room had been set with trestle tables, tended by women wearing hats and pinafores. It was strange to see so much food, and in such a setting. Not, Jessica thought, that this was anything like a real station – it even had vegetables growing on the platform, and tulips, and beyond the flaking white palings were sheep.

She overheard snatches from the waiting women.

'Only one, I told her, and not a boy, thank you!'

'Never seen soap and water for weeks, and hair crawling with lice!'

'My sister in Southport, she took two, and such little ragamuffins . . . hardly a stitch to their backs!'

'They'll have to sleep two to a bed, mind!'

There was a heavy clank as a signal changed, and the women fell silent. They watched as the engine with its plume of smoke rounded a bend and came into sight. It drew up, hissing. The stationmaster and porter hurried along the platform, wrenching open doors. At first it seemed as if the train must be quite empty, a ghost train. Its passengers were in no hurry to reach their destination.

Then, as if at a signal, the children came out, slow, reluctant. Some carried boxes, bags, bundles; others were empty-handed. Jessica, who passed such children every day in London, saw how they were changed, how scared they were and how silent. Brothers and sisters were holding hands tightly, determined to stick together in this alien land. Each child had his name pinned on his chest.

'Labelled,' thought Jessica. 'Like luggage.'

The engine hissed and birds whistled and sheep bleated. The women of Welshpool and the children from London stood uncertainly, facing one another, like armies drawn up for battle.

Jessica became aware of a small, solitary figure standing apart from the rest, beyond them. This was a child with no box, no bundle, no hand of brother or sister to hold. He seemed at that moment the loneliest child in the whole world. A cloud of steam enveloped him. As it thinned Jessica saw the boy's face, and their eyes met.

She knew those eyes. She had looked into them over a pile of smouldering rubble, against a backdrop of fire.

She gasped and took a step forward but a great cloud of steam hissed out from the engine, hiding him. When it cleared he had gone.

'He can't have!' To reach the way out he would have had to pass her. She was certain, despite the enveloping steam, that he had not. But she turned and scanned the cluster of children behind her.

'Though I wouldn't recognize him, from the back,' she realized.

'Now, children, I want you all to follow me!'

A woman who had evidently travelled with them was marshalling her charges.

'We're going to have something to eat, and then you'll all go to your new homes.'

The children shuffled into line and followed her down the platform.

'Here we are!' They filed past her. 'One, two, three – better count them,' – to one of the women waiting to serve.

'No, I shouldn't. Counted them before you left, did you?'

'Yes, of course, but –'

'Can't have *vanished*, can they? Not on a train. Come along now, children, quickly!'

Soon they were all seated. It was like a party but not a party, because faces were white and fearful. Some of the little ones were whimpering, softly, as if they knew it was hopeless.

'Will you be stopping with them, Mrs –?'

'Gray. Miss Gray. No. I have to go back tomorrow. There's another lot to come, you know.'

'Don't you fret, Miss Gray, they're safe with us, poor

lambs. As soon as they've had their food we'll get them sorted.'

'Oh, but I think I ought –'

'We've got it all arranged. Just you leave it to us. Tired out, you must be.'

'Oh – well, thank you. You're very kind.'

Jessica heard all this and wondered whether she should interrupt, tell them, 'There's one missing. Count them, and you'll see!'

But she did not. She had glimpsed the boy so fleetingly through the drifting steam that she wondered now whether she had imagined him, as Mrs Lockett insisted she had imagined the peacock.

'There's two nice little girls, Megan,' she heard Mrs Lockett say. 'Sisters they look. Pick them, I should.'

'Now, children, I want you all to get your things and make a line – don't forget your gas masks.' Megan was in charge now. 'You two – you come along with me. Stop with me, shall you?'

She pounced on the sisters she had picked for herself.

'Oh – Marlene and Gillian – there's pretty names!'

The rest of the women swooped. Jessica watched. A boy and girl, toes poking through plimsolls, eyes huge in peaked faces, grimly held fast to one another's hands as two women tried to part them.

'You come along with me now – Jimmy, is it? I've a little lad at home for you to play with.'

Dumbly he shook his head and held fast, while another woman tried to prise away his sister.

'Come along, dearie. You shall see your brother, never you fear. He won't be far away.'

The child shook her head and clung the faster. It was like a tug-of-war.

32

'We've to stop together. I'm looking after 'er. I promised my ma.'

The waiting-room was nearly empty now. The two women looked at one another helplessly.

'Oh, go on, then!' said one. 'Come with me, the pair of you. Only for now, mind. I've only room for one, I told them!'

'And what about mine?' cried the other woman, indignant. 'Where's mine?'

Jessica noticed, as they did not, one small boy left standing alone. He was knob-kneed and skinny, eyes enormous behind his thick spectacles. Against his chest he clutched a bulging carrier bag. He stood wordless, waiting to be claimed. With a pang of pity she realized that he was left because no one wanted him, skinny and pasty and plain as he was.

She touched the woman's arm.

'If you wanted a boy, there's still one left.'

'Oh – it's Trevor!' It was Miss Gray. 'Ever such a nice little lad. No trouble at all.'

'Oh, go on then. Come on then, with me.'

She nodded to him and marched out. He followed slowly. As he went, a sock fell from his carrier. Jessica picked it up.

'Here,' she said, 'you dropped this.'

He looked round and took the sock.

'Fanks.'

She smiled at him, but he had already turned away, following the woman who was to take his mother's place in this strange land.

'You're not one of mine?'

It was Miss Gray, list in hand.

'No,' said Jessica. 'I came yesterday.'

33

'On your own, are you?'

She nodded.

Miss Gray sighed.

'Oh, I don't know . . . I suppose it's all for the best.'

'Jessica's stopping with me. Up at the castle. If you'd like to come, Miss Gray, you'll be taken to where you're staying.'

'Oh, thank you.'

Jessica followed them along the platform.

'My list,' she heard Miss Gray say. 'I still haven't checked the children against my list.'

'You give it to me,' said Mrs Lockett. 'I'll see to it for you. Got everything nicely organized, don't you worry.'

'Except one thing,' Jessica thought. 'Except that boy. If there *was* a boy.'

In the station yard the bus was already full, and Miss Gray hurried forward and climbed on.

'That went nicely,' observed Mrs Lockett. She glanced at the list she had taken from Miss Gray. 'See to that later.'

She dropped it into her handbag and shut it again, click.

When they came back to the castle it seemed oppressively large and silent. Lockett went to garage the car and Jessica followed Mrs Lockett inside, where she went straight to the sink and filled the kettle.

'How many children did you say there were?' asked Jessica.

'Oh, about twenty.'

'I meant exactly.'

'Oh – about that.'

'That Miss Gray – she wanted to count them, but you all stopped her. I don't understand.'

34

'It's just an old saying here in Welshpool. Never count children twice. Ever. Heard it ever since I was little. Everybody here says it.'

'But why? There must be a reason.'

'Oh, as to reasons . . . Just a silly old story.'

'Oh, tell it to me!'

But Mrs Lockett had moved over to the wireless and turned it on. With a shock Jessica realized that here in this remote Welsh castle she was hearing exactly the same voice as she and her mother had so often heard in London. The voice was reading the news. Jessica did not want to listen. She did not put her hands over her ears, but tried to shut off the voice inside her head.

The phone rang and she jumped. Mrs Lockett answered it.

'Oh – Mrs Weaver!'

'Mum! Oh, Mum!'

'Yes . . . yes, right as rain. Yes . . . yes . . . oh, there never! Oh, I see. I see. Oh, don't you worry, Mrs Weaver.'

She was making little waving gestures to Jessica as she spoke, signs that told her to wait, that her turn would come. At last it did come. She held out the receiver and Jessica snatched it.

'Mum! Oh, Mum!'

'Jessica! Are you all right? I couldn't ring last night. There was another raid.'

'Henry – did you find Henry?'

There was a pause – long enough for Jessica to know the answer.

'You didn't!'

'Jessica, cats often disappear and then turn up. Nine lives, remember.'

Her mother was doing it again. Saying that things were all right when they weren't.

'Listen. I shan't be able to ring again, for quite a long time. I'm – going tonight.'

Jessica felt herself drowning in a slow, huge wave of fear.

'Jessica? Are you there?'

'Yes.' The voice was thin, hardly her own.

'You'll be safe where you are.'

'Yes.'

'Must go now. Only allowed two minutes. Bless you, darling. Be good. You'll find you've got everything you need in the case. Goodbye.'

'Goodbye.'

Click. Her mother had gone, gone to join her father in whatever foreign places the war was being fought. Places with no names and no landscape, unimaginable, terrible. She made for the door.

'Jessica!'

'I'm going out!'

She heard Mrs Lockett's voice follow her.

'Back by dark, mind!'

Jessica ran through the stone passageways and felt the sheer weight and size of the castle pressing in on her. It was huge and Welsh and ancient, utterly alien. Its history weighed on her like a living force.

She broke into the cool air of the courtyard, but did not stop because still she was within walls, bounded. Even when she had passed under the stone arch and was on the grassy knoll she did not stop. She ran down and through the wicket gate to the garden and turned right along a path lined with azaleas and rhododendrons, their colours glowing in the twilight.

She stopped only when she reached the pool. It lay wide and quiet, greenly reflecting and mysterious in the half light. She stood panting, and beyond her own rough breath heard the last whistles of birds echoing through all that still valley. Slowly she became aware of the peacefulness, the vast hush settling about her.

A scream tore the silence. Jessica whirled about. The peacock!

She strained into the gloom but saw nothing. Another scream, harsh, imperative.

'Where are you?'

She waited. She did not understand, but waited. Turning back to the pool she would not have been surprised to see the peacock stepping towards her over its glassy surface.

It lay calm and unbroken as before but now she saw, rising from the far bank, a white mist. As she watched, a shape appeared, moving, and it seemed to be that of a horse and rider. It came steadily on, and she realized that it was rounding the pool, coming towards her. She barely noticed that now the hush was absolute, that there was not a sound in all that valley, not the call of a bird, not even the soft drum of horses' hoofs. What she did notice was that the mist was moving with the shape it veiled.

She waited, spellbound. Now the mist was near, fingering out to touch her, icy cold. Now she saw plain the horse, white and with rich trappings, and saw too that the rider was a child. It was a young boy, pale and fair, and he looked straight at her without expression, and he was so remote and the silence was so total that it was as if they were separated by a wall of glass. He was close enough for her to reach out and touch, and yet she knew she could not.

37

He reined in his horse and sat there, sat and looked.

Jessica looked back, and at last whispered, 'Who are you?'

But the strange, wordless child gave not a flicker to show that he had heard her. He only gazed with bleak, fathomless eyes. Then his lips moved, and though there was not even the whisper of a sound she thought they framed her name – 'Jessica.' A pause, and then again the moving lips and this time she was certain – 'Jessica!'

When he had gazed his fill he gave a little jerk to the reins and the horse moved on, and with it the mist. She watched, and under her very eyes but at no particular moment and no particular place that she could point to later and say, 'There! That's where he vanished!' the mist dissolved, and horse and rider with it. They simply melted like snow. And at the moment of dissolution the birdsong flooded back and she was aware of the rank smells of undergrowth and the strong cold-water odour of the pool. It was as if the world had been holding its breath, and had now let it out again.

She hesitated, then went to the spot where she thought the boy had disappeared. She wondered if that spot was dangerous, a place where anyone, including herself, could melt and vanish. But she realized already that she did not know the exact place. The shrubs on either side were uniformly green and hung with blossom, giving nothing away.

It did not even occur to her to run, to be back safe within the thick walls of the castle. That strange, silent encounter had filled her not with fear, but with wonder. She was not even fearful that the pale boy had known her name, a certain sign that he had come, not by chance, but seeking her and her alone. Her mind was filled with a thousand questions to which she could not even guess the answers. And whatever the answers were, she was certain that she would find them not in stone rooms, but out here in the greenly breathing valley with its mists and whispers, out here where the peacock stalked.

She pondered the mystery of the peacock now as she walked back along the path and up the steps, up and up to the topmost terrace. As she wound upward she was aware of the massive, brooding presence of the ancient yews on her right hand. They were darkly enfolding secrets, had witnessed secrets centuries old and never to be spoken. Night was coming, and night was their element.

She reached the top terrace. Along the balustrade were stone urns at intervals. She counted five, faintly greenish silver in the half light. She had begun to wonder why she had climbed up there when there came the hoarse scream of a peacock close by, and she knew.

She turned to see him wheeling, tottering, balancing that great fan of feathers. Green and blue and gold, it smouldered in the dusk. She had not seen him come. He had, perhaps, made himself out of thin air, and when he went would melt like snow, as the white horse had done, and the boy rider.

'Are you really here?' she whispered. Then, 'Am I?'

She expected no answer, but it seemed that her questions had been posed to other listeners, invisible listeners who swarmed out there in the darkling valley. She heard at first only whispers.

'Jessica . . . Jessica . . . Jessica . . .'

The air was thick and crowded with her name. But the whisperers were not visible, even in a mist. The whispers faded. There was a brief silence and then, advancing, thudding feet, a gang of them and they streamed close past her as she shrank back, pressed against the cold stone. The peacock pivoted, oblivious. They almost faded and then they returned, those running footsteps, and with them came rough shouts and shrieks and she thought they must be of children, playing an invisible game of tag.

'Jessica! Jessica!'

It was a single voice, a girl's, and a pair of light footsteps scudded past. Then came heavier footsteps in pursuit, and as they came, shapes formed. She saw the outline of a chain of children, hands linked, running out of the darkness, and glimpsed the figure of a girl flying beyond them. She darted under the brick arches, then paused and looked back.

Jessica saw the girl's face, wild and desperate, for only an instant, it was barely more than a smudge in the gloom. Then the chain went thundering by and all at once there was a mist rolling along the terrace in a tide and they had all gone, last of all the peacock, vanished, quenched.

Silence. The mist thinned. There was the empty terrace, the whole printless length of it. Still Jessica did not move. She stared at the blank arches where that hunted girl had dodged barely seconds ago, and felt her skin prickle with terror.

That face she had glimpsed, eerie and impossible but unmistakable, was her own.

Four

Jessica was in a world of mist. It seemed that she carried with her a private weather, unpredictable, strange. A mist could gather, chill and white, out of a clear blue sky. It could roll out of the dawn or float in pale wreaths at twilight. And in that mist there were always children and strangest of all, those children knew her name.

That meant danger. It linked her, even against her will, with the faceless children of the mist who ran in a chain, and with the sad boy who rode on a white horse. If they knew her name, they could summon her.

The things she had seen and heard were only hints, inklings. It was as if they existed in some other dimension. They told her that she was on the edge of a mystery, but made no sense. The mist and the sightings were not connected to any particular time or place. They came to her; she could not go to them.

Yet there was a herald to these shifts between the real Powis and the Powis of the mist. The peacock. He was always there, visible in his smouldering plumage or present only as that harsh scream echoing through the whole green valley.

Or the darkness. She remembered that first night

when the scream had seemed to strike the very roof of the world. She had felt herself torn by it, and remembered that she had entered the castle in the absolute certainty that part of her remained out there in the gathering night.

And she knew now that part of her *was* out there, hunted in the mist by that running chain. But although she had seen her own face, seen her own *self*, that other Jessica had been an alien.

'I was inside me looking at her,' she thought, and faced the terrible question – who, then, was out there somewhere, her double? Who was looking at her with her own eyes?

She had woken early again, and again went out into the cool dawn. She had seen the deer, heard the cuckoo. She had neither seen nor heard the peacock. Now, as she stood gazing at the pool the first drops of rain began to fall. Its surface was at once opaque and wrinkled, reflections killed stone dead. The rain spattered on the broad leaves and the whole valley was filled with its hissing. In London, she had never thought of rain as having voices.

She began to run, making for the shelter of the orangery. As she went she realized that she liked the cool spatter of water on her skin, and half tilted her face to it and blinked as it splashed into her eyes. She ran from an old London instinct, from an umbrella world and a lifetime's warnings – 'Quick – you'll get wet!'

By the time she reached the orangery she *was* wet. Her face streamed and her hair dripped. She stood panting and looking out at a world of drenched green, and it was as if she had never seen rain properly before.

She loved the spatter of it on stone and leaf, the hiss, the whole sea sound of it.

'No mists this morning,' she thought. 'Surely not, in this!'

She hardly knew whether she was glad or sorry, because she knew that the mist was not something she could run from. Whatever strange thing had been set in motion that first night with the scream of the peacock was inevitable now. It would run its course, whether she willed or no.

Thinking of it, she remembered the blue bowl with its biscuits and apple. She turned and went swiftly over the dry stone floor to see if it were still there. That was when she saw the boy.

He lay curled against the far wall, one arm under his head to pillow it on the stone floor. Above him the stern white heads of men stared out through the streaming glass. She stood there, still at a distance, on guard. This strange sleeper in this unexpected place must surely belong to that other world of mists and children running. She scanned swiftly about her, half expecting to see other forms.

But the world held only herself and the falling and whispering rain and that single sleeping boy. She went towards him, on tiptoe, holding her breath. She was close enough to see the fall and rise of his own breathing, so close that if she had had a shadow it would have fallen over him.

Although she made not the least sound some animal instinct must have warned him of her approach, even in sleep. All at once he made a sudden, convulsive movement, and his eyes were wide open.

It was only then that she recognized him.

'You!'

He rose and crouched back against the wall, arm half shielding his face. Those eyes that had gazed at her, silvery then in his blackened face over the smoking rubble, were now wide with terror.

'What's wrong?'

'Get away!' He spat the words.

'But –'

'Get away! I can't see you – I can't!'

He buried his head then in his ragged sleeve. She was bewildered, helpless. Not knowing what to say, she waited. After what seemed an age he slowly edged his elbow down so that again she caught a glimpse of his eyes. Then they were buried again.

'Get away!' His voice was muffled.

'But why? Don't you recognize me? I do you. I saw you –'

'I *know*! And you can clear off! Stop spooking me!'

'Spooking you?'

'I ain't daft.' His head was still buried. He would not look at her.

'There's no one I know can be in two places at once!'

She began to think she saw what he meant.

'You surely don't think I'm a –'

'Can't see you and can't hear you!'

Abruptly he uncovered his face and next minute had his eyes squeezed tight shut and his fingers in his ears.

She giggled. She could not help herself.

'An' it's nuffin' to laugh at!'

'So you *can* hear me!'

'Can't!'

'So listen. I'm not some kind of a ghost, if that's what you're thinking.'

> 'Arf a pound of tuppenny rice,
> Arf a pound of treacle,
> That's the way the money goes,
> Pop goes the weasel!'

He sang tunelessly and loudly, shutting off the sound of her voice.

'All right, I'll wait.'

> 'Pack up yer troubles in yer old kit bag
> And smile, smile, smile,
> Pack up yer troubles in yer old kit bag
> And dah dah dah dah dah!'

His voice trailed off.

'Don't know the words, do you?'

> 'What's the use of worrying,
> It never was worth while,
> So pack up your troubles in your old kit bag
> And smile, smile, smile!'

She couldn't remember any more, either, and stopped. There was a silence. The rain whispered, the birds whistled.

Slowly, very slowly, he opened his eyes.

'Never 'eard of a spook *singing* . . .' He was talking to himself, rather than her.

'It's not *that* amazing, us both being here,' she told him. 'We're both –' she hesitated – 'evacuees.'

She did not want to say the word, disowned it as she said it.

'*You?* You a vacky?'

She nodded.

'Why don't you take your fingers out of your ears?'

He hesitated, then with a sheepish grimace lowered his arms.

'It's funny, I admit,' she said. 'I thought I was seeing things last night, when I —'

'That Miss Whatsit — missed me, did she?'

'No. They never even counted.'

'You sure?'

'Positive.' She giggled. 'When you disappeared in that puff of smoke I even thought I'd imagined you. Or *you* were a ghost.'

'Oh, I'm 'ere, all right.' He wandered past her to the open door and stared out into the rain. 'Worse luck.'

'Did you go over that fence?'

He nodded.

'And into that field with all them sheep. Never realized sheep was as big as that. Wasn't sure if they bit, either.'

She laughed, all at once light-headed and back to normal in this amazingly not normal situation.

'I run like stinko.'

'But why?'

'Why? Fink I was going to stop and be a vacky? No fear!' He regarded her. 'You're one. You get knocked about?'

'Of course not.'

'Get fed, then?'

'Of course.'

He pondered.

'Dead lucky, then. *I've* heard about vackys. They get put in pigsties and bashed black and blue. An' they get

46

fed on bread and water and some of 'em gets put in red
'ot baths and scrubbed *every day*!'

His look of horror made Jessica laugh again. She
could not help herself.

'Don't know why you keep larfing,' he told her, and
scowled. 'Ravenous, I am. Belly's all in knots.'

'You must be.'

She remembered then what she had been doing when
she had seen him.

'Just a minute.'

She left him and hurried down to the far end of the
orangery. There it was, the blue bowl. It was empty.

'Oh!' She gazed at it for a moment, then turned
back.

'Sorry!' she called. 'I thought –'

She broke off. The boy had gone. He was not, at any
rate, standing where she had left him.

'Hey!' she called. She realized that she did not even
know his name. 'Where are you?'

She looked about, but knew he was not there. There
was not enough greenery to hide a boy, even a skinny
one. She ran to the door and peered out, first left, then
right. She saw a shape appearing through the rain.
Without knowing why, she darted back inside and
crouched behind the door.

'He must have seen it too,' she thought.

The figure shuffled steadily on. Jessica could see that
it was an old woman with a basket. As she drew nearer,
Jessica retreated, flattening herself against the wall. She
could hear the sound of dragging feet now, beyond the
noise of rain and water. She held her breath.

'Jessica!'

The footsteps had stopped now. Whoever it was

47

knew that she was there, though she had thought herself invisible. She pressed herself harder against the wall.

'Jessica!'

A few dragging footsteps and the old woman was there before her. Jessica stared, gulped, feeling ridiculous to be discovered and to have hidden in the first place.

'Sheltering,' said the woman. 'From the rain, I dare say.'

'Yes!' Her voice was a mere squeak.

'Doing my rounds. Whatever the weather.'

She hobbled over to where the blue bowl lay empty at the foot of the ivy. From the basket she took an apple and half a loaf.

'For the children,' she said. She stooped and placed the food in the bowl.

'There!' She nudged the bowl with her foot, so that it was half hidden again by leaves. She turned.

'There's little saucers and pouches everywhere. I hide them, and the children come running.'

'What – children?' Though Jessica thought she already knew.

'Ah!' She wrapped her arms about herself and rocked. 'Hide and seek!'

Jessica stared. She could not think of a single thing to say.

'There's children in this valley dancing like moths round a candle. And running hand in hand and linked. A chain.'

Jessica swallowed.

'Do you live here? With the Locketts?'

The old woman stiffened.

'I live here! I belong here!' she hissed, and spread her arms wide. 'Mine – all mine!'

'What's – what's your name, please?'

The rain spattered.

'Ah. Not to be told. But – I'll give you a name, shall I? Not my real name, but one to call me by. What shall I say . . .? Priscilla.'

'Priscilla.'

'A whispering kind of a name . . . Priscilla.' A pause. 'Jessica . . . Jessica . . .'

The pair stood, eyes locked, in that space enclosed by rain.

'Go now, Jessica. And remember one thing. Things are not always what they seem. Say it.'

'Things are not always what they seem,' Jessica whispered.

'Good. Farewell, Jessica.'

'Farewell – I mean goodbye!'

She fled then, rushed out into the rain. Her feet threw up sparks of water. She prayed as she ran that her luck would be in, that she would catch up with the boy. But he had vanished, gone to ground.

By the time she was back in the castle she was drenched, and Mrs Lockett was there to see her.

'Just look at you, like a drowned rat! Where's your sense, girl, to go out in this?'

'It wasn't raining when I went out.'

'Pneumonia, next thing. Off with your things while I run a bath.'

Jessica obeyed. The minute she had stopped running, her wet clothes had gone cold. She had not even noticed before.

'Where's Lockett?' she asked, as a plate of bacon and

egg was put before her. 'Lovely! We hardly ever got this in London.'

'Gone out. Garden. Where else?'

'In this?'

'All weathers. If he stopped in for a drop of rain there'd be precious little done. But you'll stop in, till it clears. Got some toys to play with, have you?'

Jessica choked on her bacon.

'I'm a bit old for toys.'

'I suppose . . . Books, then?'

'A few.'

Mrs Lockett regarded her.

'I'll tell you what,' she said. 'Like to see the castle, would you?'

'Oh yes!' So far Jessica had hardly felt herself to be in a real castle at all. She had imagined sweeping staircases and crystal chandeliers, and even a few lords and ladies.

'You come along with me then, later, when I check round. Educational, it'll be.'

'I'll go and finish unpacking, then.'

Mrs Lockett was busying about the kitchen. Her eye fell on her handbag and she picked it up and opened it. From it she drew a piece of paper – the list, Jessica saw, that Miss Gray had handed to her the night before. She cast her eye over it, crumpled it and tossed it into the grate.

'That's *him* safe, then,' Jessica thought. 'Never be missed now.'

She had taken nothing from her suitcase so far except her night and wash things and the clothes she wore. Part of her had resisted. If she didn't unpack properly, it showed that she wasn't stopping, and now, for the first time, she felt she belonged here. She must belong in a place where she was known by name, as if she had been expected.

She opened a drawer and began putting things in. Her books were wedged down the sides of the case and she stacked them on top of the chest. It was good to see them, old friends and reliable. She noticed one that was unfamiliar, not looking like a proper book at all, pale cream and sprigged with flowers and leaves.

'Journal . . .' she read. She opened it and a piece of paper fluttered out. She recognized her mother's writing.

'Jessica,' she read, 'here's a book of pages for you to fill. Tell your own story!'

She sat on the edge of the bed and fanned the pages, beautifully blank, and thought, 'Of course!'

She wanted to start right away, to begin with that moment when she had stepped out into the dark and chill of the courtyard and heard that echoing scream. Fishing in her pencil case she found her fountain pen.

First, on the inside cover, she wrote her name: Jessica Weaver.

A title now . . . she sucked her pen, pondering. Then 'The Secrets of Powis Castle' she wrote, and as she did so her heart beat fast and hard. It was out in the open now, admitted, something to be reckoned with. Peacock, mists, running chain of children, all were to be plucked out of her head and set down in black and white, made part of the real world. She felt that she was doing something dangerous. She must start now, before she changed her mind.

'When I came to Powis it was nearly dark,' she

wrote. 'I got out of the car and all at once I felt cold and dizzy and then I heard a scream.'

She wrote on then, retracing her steps, unravelling the threads.

'Jessica! Ready now. Coming, are you?'

With a shock she found herself once again sitting on her bed with a pen in her hand. She had been out there on the terrace following a peacock and wandering towards a wall of mist.

'Coming!'

'Must have known I was coming, because they know my name,' she wrote.

She closed the book, hesitated, then pulling back the eiderdown, placed it under there.

At the end of the passage Mrs Lockett was already opening a door.

'Not been in a proper castle before, I dare say?'

'Not unless you count the Tower of London.'

The door swung open. Here was the vastness, the grandeur Jessica had expected. And yet, even in that first moment, she was disappointed. From the outside the castle looked magical, with its rosy stone and tumbling gardens. She had expected something gilded and graceful, the setting for a princess. These rooms were grand enough, but gloomy. They were furnished with massive pieces, shrouded in dust-sheets, standing like a sea of phantoms.

'Isn't it bare?'

'Everything been put in store, see. Safe. Look at the walls – the thickness! There's places where they're double and you can go right between, play at archers.'

Jessica saw her cue.

'You could play lots of games here,' she said, 'and outside as well. Did you . . . did you play Chain Tag?'

Mrs Lockett stopped and turned.

'Chain?'

'You know – the game where you chase and when you've caught someone you both hold hands and chase someone else. It ends up with a whole chain –'

'Fishes in a Net,' said Mrs Lockett.

Jessica stared.

'That's what we call it, round here. When there's four of you, you're to make a circle round the next one and trap him. Then he joins the chain and off you go again.'

'You did play it, then?'

'Not here. Not at the castle. Played it up in Welshpool. Oooh, scary, it was, specially if it was getting dark. Run like mad, you would. Not supposed to play it – got told off terrible if our mams found out.'

'Why?'

'Why, because –' She broke off. 'Because.'

'Was it something to do with that story you said there was – about counting children?'

Mrs Lockett moved on, and threw open the door to the next room.

'There!' She pointed to the window. 'There's Welshpool, through the trees there. Only a stone's throw, you might say.'

The wet roofs of the town shone broadly beyond the trees of the park.

'Close . . .' Mrs Lockett seemed to be talking to herself. 'Hardly a stone's throw . . . Hasn't happened, though, not for fifty years or more . . .'

'What . . . what hasn't?' prompted Jessica.

'Tommy Williams it was, that lived in the lane by the church. I can see him now – skinny and mucky he was – could've grown potatoes behind his ears. Didn't know what to do with him – his mother or the school-teacher. Up to all sorts – and never at school no matter how he got beaten. Played hookey days on end. Used to envy him . . . oh, I did . . . wished *I* dared . . .'

Jessica dared not speak but willed her to go on, to tell the story to its end.

'Played it once too often, though. Poor Tommy . . .' she sighed. 'Went truant for once and all . . .'

'You mean . . .?'

'Never came back.'

A clock was ticking heavily in the depths of the room somewhere. Jessica had not noticed it before.

'That was when they got rid of the peacocks.'

Jessica held her breath. She did not want to break the spell. She knew that she was on the very verge of the mystery.

'Why?' she whispered.

'Tommy – before he disappeared – he was always talking about them. Used to quiz him, we did, about where he'd been. "I follow the peacock," he'd say. Thought he was daft.'

'But I don't see . . .'

'It was a peacock before. All those hundreds of years ago.'

Jessica waited.

'A little lordling. Fair as the day, the story says. And the Green Lady wanted him for her own.'

Her voice was soft and weaving, lost in telling its story.

'And she sent a peacock, they say, to lure him.' She

54

turned. 'Just a lot of old nonsense, I expect. The whole story.'

'But what story?'

'Oh, I haven't time. Ask Lockett. Believes in it still, he does, which is more than I do!'

'You believed in it enough to get rid of that list,' Jessica thought.

Five

'Find Lockett, or find *him*,' Jessica told herself, meaning the boy. 'Oh, why didn't I ask his name?'

If only she had, she could have called it until he recognized her voice and came. He was hungry, she knew that. He could have gone back to Welshpool in search of food. He could have been seen and caught and sent to somebody's house, like all the other children, the evacuees.

'Vackys,' she thought. Then, 'That's it! Don't know his name, but I'll call him "Vacky"!'

She reached for her journal.

'Off to look for vacky,' she wrote, 'taking food.'

She went in search of it.

'Please can I have something to eat, Mrs Lockett?' she rehearsed. 'I'm ravenous, I'll never last till dinnertime.'

She need not have bothered. She pushed open the kitchen door and saw that the room was empty. On the table was a rack with scones cooling. Jessica ran to the cupboard and took down a bowl. Into it went three scones. Then into the larder, cold and smelling of stone. Bread. She tore a wing from a cooked chicken, snatched up an apple.

Her heart was thudding as she escaped into the courtyard. The rain had stopped and now the sun was out, flashing on the wet stone. She followed the path down into the garden to begin her search.

'Vacky! Vacky!' she called, softly at first, but then louder, emboldened by the thought that there was no one else to hear her, except perhaps Lockett. She went along the terraces, up and up, calling. She passed the seven brick arches, peered into the deserted orangery.

'Vacky! Vacky!'

She stood on the topmost terrace and wheeled, scanning the scene below. He could be anywhere, she thought, could be in the huge park, hiding with the deer.

She did not give up. She went on searching because there was nothing else in the whole world to do, nothing that had any point. She wanted to find him to feed him, because he was hungry and because he was the only friend she had. And beyond those reasons, though she did not put the thought into words, was the feeling that he and she were destined to meet. Why else would their eyes have met over that smouldering rubble, and again through the drift of steam at the station? Jessica was looking for him because she knew that they shared the same story.

Down she went, down the steps and the sloping path that led through the tunnel of yew.

'Vacky! Vacky!'

'Boo!'

She shrieked and dropped the bowl. It shattered at her feet. There he was, grinning.

'Why did you do that?' she wailed. 'Now look!'

He looked and his eyes fixed on the scattered food.

57

Then he was snatching it up, cramming it into his mouth, wolfish. She watched, amazed, wondering how hungry you had to be to feed off the ground. He tore at the bread, gnawed at the chicken wing.

'What's your name? I don't know your name.'

He seemed not to hear her. He bit and chomped and swallowed. The food was vanishing fast, was nearly all gone.

'Thank you very much, Jessica,' she said. 'It was kind of you to remember me!'

'You what?' Mouth full.

'Nothing. Why'd you run off like that?'

He surveyed her, head cocked.

'*You* ain't a vacky!'

'I am, then.'

'You talk too posh!'

She laughed.

'All right, then – where d'yer live?'

'There.' She pointed up at the castle. His eyes popped, disbelieving.

'In the castle?'

'With the Locketts.'

'First I've 'eard of vackys in blooming great castles! Is there a dook in there, or what?'

'P'raps. I don't know. Listen – I'm Jessica. Jessica Weaver.'

He looked at her, alert, suspicious. She waited.

'What's your name?'

'Don't 'ave to tell!'

'Course you don't. But you'd better if we're going to be friends.'

Still no answer.

'Or if I'm going to bring you food,' she added.

'Billy,' he said grudgingly.

'Billy what?'

'Nuff for now. There's millions of Billys.'

'I expect there are,' she agreed.

'And I ain't calling you Jessica, neither! Jessica!' he scoffed. 'Soppy name! Vacky, ain't yer? I'll call yer that!'

'Where did you sleep last night?'

Again that shuttering of his face.

'In the orangery?'

No reply.

'You'd better look out. There's a barmy old woman about.'

'Her that came this morning?'

'Yes.'

'She see you? I didn't arf skedaddle off quick – bet you never saw me!'

'It doesn't matter if she sees me. I live here.'

'Ooh yes – forgot! Queen of the blooming castle, lah de dah de dah!'

'All I'm saying is – look out.'

'Saw her before you did.'

That was true. He was probably used to ducking and diving among those narrow, sooted streets not far from where she lived. She had seen plenty like him, pinching apples from stalls as they ran, the whole world their playground. She knew quite certainly that Billy was from one of those gangs of mucky children her mother had told her not to speak to, let alone play with. She had been quite scared of them, would never have ventured into their territory alone. On that morning after the raid she had not known what she was doing or where she was going.

'Did you?' she persisted. 'Sleep in the orangery?'

'Not telling.'

'It'd be safer in Welshpool.'

He jumped to his feet.

'Tara, vacky!'

He was up and running, and she went after him.

'Billy! Where're you going?'

'Welshpool.'

'Wait! Billy, wait!'

He spun round.

'What?'

'I just –'

She had meant to warn him, warn him of mists, of running chains of children, of peacocks. Now, in the broad light of day, it seemed impossible.

'I just – I'll bring you some more food!'

'Get some in Welshpool.'

'But – they'll see you.'

He shrugged.

'Don't matter. There's dozens of vackys.'

It was true. Welshpool had been invaded by strange children, no one knew one from another – and no one knew how many. No one had ever counted them and no one ever would. Billy might as well be invisible.

'But you can't run away for ever!'

His face was pinched, his eyes hardened.

'Can't I! Can't I just! Fink I'm living in a pigsty and beat black and blue?'

'It's not true! You wouldn't be!'

'Sez you! No fanks! Toodleoo!'

He was off again. Helplessly Jessica watched him go.

'He's all alone,' she thought. 'Worse than me, even.'

He turned.

'Might even go back to London!' he bawled. 'Put that in your pipe and smoke it!'

He turned again.

'No!' she called after him. 'Don't! Please!'

He kept running, a tiny figure in the wide meadow. She watched till he disappeared.

She was alone again. She raised her eyes to the pink stone of the castle, and saw how foreign it was, how unlike home. She sat down and shut her eyes and tried to conjure up her own home. All she saw was that gashed wall, those tilting floors and cracked ceilings. She had no home. Even if she ran off, went back to London, there was nowhere to go. She saw again her father in his khaki on the swarming station. He had gone off to that mysterious place called the Front. And her mother . . . she could not even begin to imagine where she might be. Driving an ambulance, for the wounded. Where there were casualties there was danger . . . the Front! Her father and mother were both at the Front!

A scream rang through the quiet gardens. Jessica opened her eyes. She saw a green blur and then, blinking, the jewelled blue of the peacock. He stood swaying.

'You aren't there,' she whispered. 'There are no peacocks.'

He did not vanish as she had half expected. Instead, a milky white mist made itself, and she heard her name whispered.

'Jessica . . . Jessica . . .'

She knew that voice, it was as if she had spoken her own name and it was given back to her as an echo.

'Jessica . . . Jessica . . .' the voice coaxed and drew

61

her. She took a few faltering steps forward, frightened but irresistibly drawn.

Then the figure of a girl took shape and it was as if Jessica were looking into a mirror through a cloud of steam. There stood herself yet not herself. She was looking straight into her own eyes. *Or was it the other way round?*

That other she was watching her intently. She did not appear terrorstruck by meeting her own double. She seemed almost to have expected it, made it happen, even. Her look was chill and mocking.

'That's not me, that's not me,' said a voice inside Jessica's head.

But it was. It was the Jessica she knew from the looking-glass, now with a life of her own. As if to prove it, she stretched out a hand.

For an instant Jessica was drawn, tempted to put out her own hand and –

'No! No!'

She heard her own scream as she turned and fled. She did not look behind to see if she was being followed, or whether the mist had come down again. She ran and ran and wanted to be running home, back to where it was safe and familiar. She wanted to run in through her own front door, to see the worn brown carpet and the hatstand and Henry lying in the warm patch by the stairs.

When she stopped running because her breath had gone, she was still in the garden, still a hundred miles from home. And that garden, for all its quiet and greenness, was a dangerous place.

'Like the Front.'

The Front, where her father was and her mother too, for all she knew, was a place where people went and sometimes never came back. Here, children were tiptoe-ing along the very edge of the world, it seemed. Mists formed, rough children went running in a chain, a peacock screamed.

'Poor Tommy – went truant for once and all. Never came back . . .'

Children disappeared.

'Just an old story in Welshpool. Never count children twice. Never.'

She herself was here, but somewhere out there, too. She counted as one, but it seemed that there were two of her.

'But not really. She isn't me. I was looking at her with my eyes, not looking at me with hers. So – who was looking at me?'

She felt dizzy, her head ached. The sum would not add up. She actually clutched her head with both hands, as if to force an answer from it.

'Oh! Oh! I feel like screaming!' The words came out tight and gritted. 'What am I doing here?'

She did not know. She had been sent here. No one had asked her whether she minded. She did mind, terribly. She could hardly bear it.

'Jessica?'

The voice was soft but she jumped, her hands flew out.

'Ah!' It was Lockett, surveying her with a strange look as if he, too, had seen a ghost.

'*Am* I a ghost?' she wondered, and half meant it.

'I thought . . . just for a minute . . .'

'What?'

'You looked – stonestruck.'

'*What?*'

63

'Nothing. It don't mean nothing. All right, are you?'

'Course.'

There was no other answer possible. How to tell him of mist and peacock and that awful mirror self? And yet . . . what was it he had said? He knew about the peacock, said there was a story, a story that gathered power with the telling.

'Lockett . . .?'

He looked at her and she saw how safe he was, and rooted. In his trousers, braces and big black boots he had walked and worked the gardens of Powis and no harm had come to him. He sowed seeds, and dug, and lopped trees, and was well and truly in this world and of it. He would not swerve aside from a stalking peacock or jostling chain of boys.

'Tell me the story.'

'I knew you'd be asking me,' he said.

'About the little lordling and the Green Lady.'

'Long ago,' he said, 'and takes some believing.'

'I'll believe it.'

'Oh yes. Seeing is believing. Right, am I?'

She knew what he meant.

'Yes. The peacock.'

'Heard *and* saw?'

She nodded.

'Ripe for the picking . . .' He said it to himself. 'Look, sent here to be safe, you were.'

'I know,' she said miserably. She marvelled again at the blindness of grown-ups who could think that anywhere but home was safe.

'There's no one knows the whole story. There's no one can.' He paused. 'And there's some don't want to believe it. Not nowadays. You get *real* magic, like aeroplanes and the wireless, and they don't want talk of any Green Lady.'

'But they *know*! Mrs Lockett said —'

'Tommy Williams. He was the last.'

'But why?'

'She stole the lordling — Harry, his name was, and skin as white as milk. She wanted him for her son. But it won't mix, flesh and blood and stone. That's what she had, see — has. A heart of stone.'

'So . . . what happened?'

'He was lonely. He wanted another child of flesh and blood, as friend. Made a vow — of silence. Said that he would never utter a word until he had one.'

The boy by the pool, Jessica was thinking. The sad-faced silent boy on the white horse.

'And that's why she stole all those other children — for him?'

'But they say, too, that he whispered a name.'

Jessica . . . Jessica . . . Jessica . . .

'What — name?'

'Who can tell? Only him — and her.'

'And me,' Jessica thought.

'There's always someone can break a spell.'

They were both silent for so long that when he suddenly spoke again she jumped.

'I'll tell you two things. The Green Lady. Beautiful, they say, with golden hair and a smiling face on her you'd never guess her badness. But she can change her shape.'

'What do you mean?'

'She can appear as anyone at all. Old, young, dark, fair . . .'

'What's the other thing?'

'Mind what you wish!'

'You said that before. What does it mean?'

'Your wishes are part of her power. The Green Lady.'

'What?'

'There was a boy once, long ago, disappeared for days. Then back he came, half crazed. Babbling about peacocks and running chains of children.'

'Tommy!'

'No – before that – another boy. He'd run off from home – wished himself gone. And with the wishing, she'd half got him.'

'Half?'

'Then all that was left was for the others to catch him. Fish in a net.'

Those thundering feet, that terrified girl – herself.

'They came after him, all the other children, in and out of nights and days and always in a mist.'

'And – if they'd caught him?'

'Stonestruck.'

'*What?*'

'Hers. Heart turned to stone.' There was a small silence. 'I've frightened you.'

'Yes.'

'Meant to, I s'pose. You away from home, and all. Might . . . might wish yourself away from here . . .'

It was too late. She already had. That first night, as she climbed from the car and saw the great bulk of the castle looming above her. She had stood shivering in the foreign darkness and the peacock had let out his scream of triumph.

'I'm half-way there,' she thought. 'Stonestruck . . .'

Six

It was the first time Jessica had gone to Welshpool alone and on foot. She had not known the world was so big, or so empty, so quiet.

'Might as well be on the moon,' she thought.

Her whole life had been spent among houses and people and noise. In London things were always happening; all you had to do was go along with it, be swept into it. Here, it was as if the world was a blank white paper. *You* had to write on it. You had to make things happen.

'I'm homesick,' she thought. And then, almost at once, 'Mind what you wish!'

She tried not to wish herself back in the busy streets, but the effort was enormous. The more she tried the harder it was.

'You can't stop wishes!'

It was as if they had a life and power of their own. They sprang from deep, secret places in your head, and were there before you knew it.

'You don't wish wishes, they wish you!'

The thought was so frightening that she started to run. She had not meant to. She had meant to go slowly, cautiously, keeping her eyes open for the deer.

As she ran she fixed her sight on the town ahead with its reassuring rows of roofs and chimneys.

But when she left the park behind and was once more on solid ground she was still in a strange land. There were streets and houses, cars and bicycles, but even the people seemed oddly slow, like clockwork toys not properly wound up.

She went past the houses with their victory gardens – rows of cabbages and carrots instead of flowers.

'Not really expecting bombs here, though.'

None of the windows had the criss-crossed brown bands of tape to prevent flying glass. These houses were safe – safe as houses.

'It's not fair!'

On the step of a house ahead she saw a small figure hunched. He raised his head as she went by and she saw that it was the boy who had been last to be chosen at the station. He sat hugging his bony knees, eyes owl-like behind the pebble lenses.

'Hello! Trevor?'

He looked at her but did not answer.

'I saw you at the station, remember? Picked your sock up.'

No reply.

'You all right?'

It was a silly question. He was obviously not all right, hunched in mute misery on that stone step. There came a chanting in the distance.

'Fleas, fleas – evacuees! Fleas, fleas – evacuees!'

'Bye!'

She waved and ran and rounded the corner and there they were. A group of children were watching two girls playing hopscotch on the pavement.

'Fleas, fleas – evacuees!'

'Shut up!' The older girl turned and faced her tormentors. 'Shut your face – fleas yourself!'

'Mucky beggars!'

'Nits in your hair!'

'Who wet her knickers?'

Shrieks of laughter.

'Shut *up*!' She threw the stone she was holding.

'Owch!' A boy clapped a hand over his eye. 'Oooch, oooch!'

'Serve you right!' she spat. The younger girl clung to her.

Still the boy groaned.

'Now look what you've done!'

'Blinded him!'

'You'll be for it!'

'Don't care!' She stood her ground, daring them.

'Now what? What's all this?'

A woman rushed out of her house, still wiping her hands on her pinafore. It was Megan, Mrs Lockett's friend.

'It's her – that mucky vacky!'

'Throwing stones – could've blinded him!'

The boy struck by the stone renewed his moans.

'Little madam!' The woman took a swipe at her and just caught the top of her head as she sprang back.

'You *stop* that!' The smaller girl ran at the woman and kicked her shins, hard. Jessica almost cheered.

'Oooh – little devil!'

'C'mon – run!'

The pair fled with the speed of practice, learned in the network of narrow streets they came from.

'Just you wait!' shrieked the woman after them. 'Little guttersnipes!'

Jessica looked at the group of Welsh children. They were grinning and tittering – especially the boy who had been hit by the stone. He had dropped his hand, and she saw that he was not hurt at all – visibly, at least. The stone had probably not even struck him. She hesitated, then went after the girls.

She went as fast as she could without running. If they looked over their shoulders, she did not want them to think she was pursuing them.

'Just keep sight of them. Bound to catch up in the end.'

When she did the pair had flopped down and were sitting on the deep kerb, literally in the gutter. The little one was sniffing and the other had her arm round her.

'Shut up now, Gilly. 'S all right.'

'I want to go 'ome!' – the last word a rising howl.

'Well, you can't. Ain't no use snivelling.'

'I hate her!'

''Orrible old bleeder,' the other agreed. 'Least we're togevver, Gilly.'

'Oh, Marlene! How long've we to stop?'

'Dunno.'

'Hello,' said Jessica.

They jumped, startled, and looked up at her, grubby faces streaked and tear-stained.

'Who're you?' demanded Marlene.

'Jessica. Jessica Weaver. I'm a vacky, too.'

'Hard cheese, then!' retorted Marlene. Then, suspiciously, 'Don't look like one.'

'Well, I am. As a matter of fact the person I'm

staying with is friends with the one you're with – Megan.'

'Mrs Jones? What, on our street?'

'Not – exactly.'

As she stood above them Jessica was aware of a sickly smell. She knew what it was. One of them *had* wet her knickers. Her mother, she knew quite certainly, would not approve of her talking to these children. But her mother was a million miles away. This was here and now, and she needed friends – any friends.

'That was a jolly good kick you gave her!'

'Serve 'er right!'

'Says we've got fleas!'

'And nits!'

Looking at them, Jessica was not surprised. She thought they probably had. What was more, she did not care.

'Said we wasn't proper little girls at all! Said she wanted *proper* girls!'

'What – with bows in their hair? Sugar and spice and all things nice?' Jessica giggled and herself sat down on the kerb beside them.

'Like to put a *bomb* up 'er bottom!'

The pair clutched one another and rolled with mirth. Jessica, deliciously shocked, shrieked with them.

'You're lucky,' she said. 'At least you've got each other.'

'Here – you sure you're a vacky? Don't talk like one.'

'Well, I am. And don't say I'm posh because I'm not.' She paused. 'If I tell you where I'm stopping, promise you won't call me posh?'

They stared at her, waiting.

'See that?' She pointed. The castle was visible beyond the trees.

'What – that blooming great palace?'

'Castle. Yes – there.'

'What – wiv the king and queen?' Gilly was awestruck.

'No, silly. I told you. A friend of Mrs Jones.'

'You're fibbing!'

'I'm not!'

'Are!'

'Not!'

'C'mon, Gilly!' Marlene tugged at her and they jumped to their feet and ran. At a distance they paused.

'Liar, liar, your knickers on fire!'

Gilly stuck her tongue out and the pair turned on their heels and ran. Jessica, still sitting in the gutter, watched them go. There was no point in going after them, not now. But she knew their names and they hers, and they would meet again.

'Jessica! Whatever?'

She jumped up. It was Mrs Lockett.

'I – I came to find you. Carry your shopping.'

'Oh well, as to that, not a lot to carry. Never is, these days. Here.'

She handed over the basket.

'Been to see Mrs Jones – my friend Megan. Having a terrible time, she says.'

'Why?' asked Jessica, knowing the answer.

'Those two girls – remember she picked at the station? Terrible! Proper little guttersnipes.'

'What *are* guttersnipes? I thought snipes were birds. You don't get birds –'

'Mucky, she says – underwear you wouldn't believe!

And nits in their hair. You keep away from them, Jessica.'

It was probably too late. She had sat giggling with them in the gutter.

'And – you'll never believe – wet her bed, the little one did!'

'And her knickers!' Jessica thought.

'Seven years old and wet her bed. Done it o' purpose, Meg says, to spite her.'

All the way back to the castle Mrs Lockett kept up a steady flow. The evacuees should never have been sent, not to a nice place like Welshpool. She had never been to London, and if that was the way people brought up their kiddies she didn't want to, thank you very much. You could hardly imagine the kind of homes they came from.

'Not you, of course, dear. From a nice home you are, I know that. And a lovely mother. I told Megan. Lucky I am, I told her, mine's ever so nice.'

'Thank you,' said Jessica wanly.

They were in the shadow of the castle when she spotted Billy. He crouched by a tree, quite still, staring at a group of deer near by.

'The deer! Never seen them in the day before.'

'Oh, you will, dear, living here.' Mrs Lockett did not even glance at them. 'Part of the furniture, you might say.'

'I – could I go and look?'

'You'll not get very close,' Mrs Lockett warned, and took the basket.

Jessica advanced slowly, wary both of Billy and the deer. She was half-way there when one of them lifted his head. Then he was off, and the others with him. She started to run. Billy, pale and wide-eyed, stayed as he was.

'Fanks.' Then, grudgingly, 'Not bad for a girl.'

'What?' She was mystified.

'Blooming great fings. Thought I was a gonner.' He stared after them. 'What *are* they?'

Suddenly she understood. Billy, who had never realized how big sheep were, and was frightened even of them, had been terrified by these other outsized beasts.

'Deer. But why did you get so close to them?'

'Didn't! No fear! Asleep, wasn't I? Open me eyes, and there they are!' He shuddered. 'Fanks. 'Ere – there ain't any lions and tigers?'

'Course not, silly. And deer won't hurt you – the other way round – they're scared of us.'

'Garn!' He did not believe it. He looked glumly about him at the wide, sunwashed park. 'Ain't it big – and quiet! Where's all the 'ouses?'

'It's the country.'

'Well, I don't like it. Fact, I 'ates it. Gets on yer nerves.'

'Come on – let's go to the garden. Under those arches.' She was coaxing him, as she would have lured the deer had she had the chance. 'More like home.'

But when they reached the terraces and the orangery Billy seemed no happier. He prowled restlessly about, kicking at the stone with his ramshackle boots. Jessica became aware that he, too, was smelly.

'Hates it, hates it, hates it!'

'You're just homesick. So 'm I.'

'Home!' He whirled about. 'What home?'

'Mine's gone as well. Was that yours – the one burning that day?'

74

He nodded.

'Where's your mother?'

His face twisted, he raised both hands. She thought for a moment he was going to hit her. Then he had flung himself face downward on the ground and was writhing, fists beating, shoulders shaking. His sobs were terrible, painful, as if forced out of him against his will.

'Oh no!' Jessica whispered.

She knelt by him and timidly touched his shoulder.

'Don't! Don't!'

'And Frank! And Queenie! Oh oh oh!' He beat his fists on the ground. 'Them bloody Jerries! That bloody Hitler!'

'Oh, Billy!' She stared down helplessly. She saw again those fiery houses, those smouldering heaps of rubble, could smell them, almost.

'Jessica! Jessica!'

She jumped to her feet, relieved and ashamed of it.

'Got to go! Back later!'

She ran a few paces then turned back.

'Bring you some food. Don't go, Billy – don't!'

He lay, sobbing, and did not reply. She hurried up towards the castle, her mind crowded with burning houses.

'Poor Billy! Oh, poor Billy!'

His mother had been in that rubble, dead. Frank and Queenie, she guessed, were his brother and sister. She had thought what had happened to her was the worst thing in the world. It was not. The worst thing in the world had happened to Billy.

'And what'll he be wishing?'

He was adrift in the grounds of Powis and did not know that he, too, was under threat. His heart was already broken. Perhaps it was only a hair's breadth from being . . .

'Stonestruck!'

She stopped dead.

'And there's part of me out there – looking like me! What if – what if she finds him, and Billy thinks she's me!'

For an instant she was tempted to turn and run back.

'Jessica!'

Mrs Lockett was standing on the path above her.

'Hurry up now, dear. Dinner's ready.'

She turned and went, and Jessica stumbled obediently after her.

Seven

Jessica had barely left the courtyard of the castle when the peacock screamed. The sound rang thin and piercing as if in frost. Was it possible that Mrs Lockett in her warm kitchen and Lockett in his garden did not hear it?

The peacock waited, then wheeled and trod away and Jessica knew she was meant to follow. She had come straight out after dinner to find Billy, and warn him of the spell that bound the valley. Instead she found herself drawn after the bird who seemed to come as messenger, as go-between. He alone could freely come and go between then and now, that world and this.

He led her down the sloping path and then, instead of turning along the terrace, went down further, along the shady path towards the pool. Down they went, between the overhanging shrubs, and Jessica's heart hammered because she thought she knew why.

The pool lay green and glassy. Along its rim, as she had expected, moved a milky white mist.

'This time I'll make him speak,' she thought. 'I know his name now. Harry.'

She stood and watched the mist move towards her.

Then it dissolved, and there he was, the small fair boy on a white horse. But he was not alone. Leading him was a lady with long golden hair and streaming robes. She was beautiful and terrifying, her skin too white, eyes aglitter.

'The Green Lady!' Jessica would have run, but her feet seemed rooted.

'Here she is, my darling,' said the Green Lady softly. 'I fetched her for you.'

The boy's eyes looked straight into Jessica's.

'She's the one you've waited for. Say her name. Say it!'

The boy's lips moved.

'Jessica!' he whispered.

'Shall I steal her for you? Shall I?'

He seemed not to hear, his gaze still fixed on Jessica. Now the Green Lady looked at her too, and smiled. The smile was cold and careful.

'Speak to him,' she said.

Dumbly Jessica shook her head. She could not move and she could not speak.

'Ah, cruel . . .' the lady sighed. 'It's you he's dreamed of all these years, century in and century out. Speak to him, won't you?'

Her voice was coaxing, wheedling.

'Shouldn't you like to come and live with us? It's beautiful here . . . beautiful . . . everything you wished for I'd give you, and you'd stay a child for ever . . . like Harry.'

Still Jessica was frozen. She could not speak, dared not.

'You speak to her, Harry. Ask her.'

He moved his lips, but at first no sound came.

'He's been dumb for centuries,' Jessica thought. 'He's forgotten how to speak.'

Then slowly, painfully, he did speak.

'Jessica . . .' he said again. 'It's true. I've waited for you. Waited and waited . . .'

'And now she's here, my darling,' crooned the Green Lady. 'Ask her! Ask her!'

'I waited —' he paused — 'for you to — break the spell!'

'What?' hissed the Green Lady, and her fair face twisted.

'Don't listen to her, Jessica! If you're brave enough — save me, save me!'

'No!'

The Green Lady screamed and she raised an arm and seem to comb down mist with her long white fingers. Next minute she, the boy and the horse were lost in its dense swirl.

'Save me! Save me!'

The cries faded. The mist cleared. The bank of the pool was empty.

The peacock?

He, too, had gone, treading back into whatever darkness he came from.

'What did he mean?' she whispered. 'Save me! What did he mean — if you're brave enough?'

She thought of the chain of rough children, heard their thudding feet. She shivered.

'I'm a coward.'

Till now, only her mother and herself had known this. Why had that lonely boy waited for her through the centuries?

'There's always someone who can break a spell.' That was what Lockett had said.

'But why me, why me?'

She could not tell. She had been drawn into his story against her will. She had been given a part she did not want to play. She did not even know how to play it.

'It wouldn't surprise me,' she thought, 'if my hair turned grey!'

She laughed at herself then, out loud. She did not know what to do to save Harry, but at least she could find Billy, warn him.

'If he disappears, no one'll know, except me. He was never counted.'

Billy could melt into that spellbound valley and vanish without trace. If once that happened, it would be beyond her power to save him. He would be stonestruck.

'And in her power – for ever.'

She ran first along the terraces, calling his name. She peered under the brick arches and into the orangery. When she reached the top she stood by the balustrade, scanning the valley. It was a world apart, a green, mysterious world crammed with invisible and secret presences.

Far below she saw Lockett moving slowly along the rows of his victory garden.

'He knows about the Green Lady and the peacock, but he hasn't seen them. He doesn't belong in the story.'

She looked sideways at the leaden figure poised in mid-dance, frozen at one particular step in time.

'Pity you can't talk!' she told it, and went.

She went to the dusty, shadowy shelter of the great yew hedge where Billy had jumped out at her earlier. He was not there, nor had she expected him to be.

'Won't be in the park, either, not hiding, anyway. Too scared of the deer.'

Jessica went down the wide, shallow steps by the yew hedge, and halted at the bottom. She looked uncertainly about. To her left were the formal and the victory gardens, and Lockett. To her right, and beyond a wide, grassy stretch, was what looked like a wilderness of trees and shrubs.

'Could be in there somewhere.'

She hesitated. Here, close to the castle and along the terraces, despite the chain of children and the stalking peacock, she felt safe – or almost safe. The Locketts might appear at any moment.

But at the heart of the mystery were the pale boy on the white horse and the Green Lady herself. She had seen them only in the dark shrubbery by the pool – right out of sight and hearing of any other human being.

'And now the Green Lady's seen me. She thinks I can save Harry. She'll be after me!'

She shivered under the hot sun. She saw again that narrow white face, those icy eyes. That woman who had spells at her fingertips could be waiting for her in that far wilderness.

'If you're brave enough – save me, save me!'

Already the valley was thronged with children caught in the net, gone for ever from their old lives. They were invisible now, almost impossible to imagine in this wide and sunlit place. But Jessica had heard their thundering, printless feet, been brushed by the icy draught they made. She had glimpsed them as they streamed out of the darkness. They knew her name.

'I'm sorry, Harry,' she whispered. 'I daren't!'

She turned and began the climb back up towards the castle. Even now she hoped that Billy was hiding, would come out.

As she went again past the dim hidey-hole under the yew she remembered the hidden food. She went in, smelling the dry dust of centuries. There it was, the net, and in it apples. She could not make sense of it. Why should that old woman feed the children? They were invisible – how could she know of them?

'For the children,' said a soft voice.

Jessica spun about. There she was, the bent crone with her basket filled with bread and cake and apples.

'Here!' She held out an apple.

Jessica shook her head.

'Take it, dearie. There's plenty for all.'

'I – I'm not hungry.'

'Put it in your pocket. It's rarely juicy.'

'I – don't like apples,' she lied.

'A little cake then. Here . . .' and she rummaged in her basket. 'A cake for Jessica!'

Suddenly Jessica knew how the old woman knew her name. She stared into the criss-crossed face and beneath it saw another, unearthly white. She heard Lockett's voice: 'She can change her shape, appear as anyone at all.'

Jessica drew a deep breath.

'No, thank you. I'm not hungry.'

And she went past the old woman so close that she almost brushed her, and felt her skin crawl.

She ran up and along the terrace, past the orangery and the leaden peacock. She would not have stopped if that peacock had come to life, stepped into her path with gaudy fan and tilted head. She ran up the path, across the courtyard, into the castle and the safety of her room.

She sat heaving for breath. She looked about her, seeing with relief her own familiar things, her hairbrush, photos, books, anchoring her to her past life. She stared at the picture of her younger self with her mother and father. Her salvaged toothbrush lay there and she clutched it and held it tight as if it were a charm.

She wished she could stay here for ever, till the war was over and the world back to normal. She did not want ever to go into those dangerous gardens again.

'I needn't. I can stay round the house – the castle.'

There was only another week before her friends would arrive, the whole school, and there would be gossip and games and giggling.

'Never thought I'd ever be glad for term to start,' she thought, and smiled.

Her eye fell on the decorated cover of the book where she was writing her story.

'Might as well do that. Tell what happened today.'

And so she did. She wrote it all – the visit to Welshpool and meeting Gilly and Marlene. Billy, frightened by deer and later convulsed by grief. She wrote the story Lockett had told her, and then the appearance of the peacock and the strange meeting by the pool. Lastly, her heart thudding as she remembered it, she told of the second meeting with Priscilla.

'She's the Green Lady, really, I know she is,' she wrote. 'But she won't get me. She can't. I don't *want* to break the spell. I live in London, and it's nothing to do with me. I'm stopping where it's safe till the rest of the school comes.'

She re-read what she had written.

'That's it, then. I'll write THE END. That'll finish it!'

She nodded, and picked up her pen. As she did so she heard the telephone ring.

'Could be Mum!'

She dropped the book and hurried out and along the stone passage to the kitchen. She could hear Mrs Lockett's voice, oddly high. She paused by the half-open door.

'Oh, you never! Oh dear, oh dear!'

It was not her mother. It was some kind of bad news.

'Oh, I'm so sorry . . . well, of course . . . no, no I won't – not a word. Poor child.'

Jessica, about to go back to her room, paused. Child – what child? Billy?

'No, she's settled in lovely . . . no . . . no point at all telling her. Oh, poor child!'

Jessica leaned against the door frame, suddenly sick and dizzy.

'Oh dear, this dreadful war . . . will it never end . . .?'

Blindly she turned and stumbled away.

Eight

Jessica went to the garden, her earlier resolution forgotten. Even had she remembered, she would not have cared.

There was news too terrible to tell her, and she had heard it. Usually, of course, such news came by telegram. She had heard the women talking.

'Oh well, mustn't grumble. As long as there's no telegram – that's the main thing.'

Jessica went blindly past the blind statues, going nowhere. She could taste salt on her lips. Her limbs felt strangely heavy, as if she were walking in water, wading through air.

'London Bridge is falling down falling down, falling down
London Bridge is falling down, my fair lady.'

The refrain ran in her head, came of its own accord, to stop her from thinking. She did not want to think, somehow she must put off the moment when she would have to. There were certain terrible words that threatened to surface, words she could not bear. One unthinkable thing had already happened – her home had gone.

Now another . . . now another . . .

She put her hands over her ears as if that would prevent her hearing words inside her own head.

'London Bridge is falling down falling down falling down . . .'

She could not keep it up for ever. She could not keep walking for ever. There was no way out. Sooner or later she would have to turn and meet the pain.

'Oh, I wish, I wish – no, I don't wish!'

When the peacock screamed, it was as if he were screaming out the pain of the whole world.

She stopped. There he was, a blur of blue and green and gold, and suddenly she loved him, because he was outside time, outside the world. He was playing his part in a story that had nothing to do with war, the Front, telegrams – death. In that instant, staring at his stiffly tilted head, Jessica chose that story.

Only an hour ago she had run from it, choosing ordinariness and safety. Now there was no safety. Wherever that story led her at least there was a part to play, the possibility of a happy ending. If it led her out of the world for ever, it hardly mattered now.

The peacock scuffed and swayed. He did not, as she had expected, turn and lead her. Jessica brushed her sleeve across her eyes and looked beyond him.

There, impossibly, veiled in a thin mist, were herself – and Billy. They stood at a short distance, watching her.

'That is not me,' she told herself carefully. '*But is that Billy?*'

She had no way of knowing. Billy could have wished himself away, as she herself had, all unknowing, on that first night. He could already be half-way to being stonestruck. Or could that be the real Billy with her own double, thinking her real?

Her eyes met those of the other Jessica. There was no flicker of response. Then her double pulled at Billy's sleeve and ran, he after her.

'No!' Jessica gasped.

Then the mist came down. It hid the running figures in a white swirl. She started to run.

'No!' she screamed. 'Billy – no!'

But above the thud of her own footsteps she heard others, thundering fast, nearer, nearer. The chain of stonestruck children was coming. She heard their yells and shouts and ran as she had never run before. They were playing Fishes in a Net, and she was fish.

'Catch her!'

'Get her!'

She fled from the badness of them, the spiteful chattering. Then her foot caught on a stone and she fell.

'Now!' she thought. It was the end.

She lay on the cold turf and fleetingly wondered how it would feel to be stonestruck. She lay and waited to be encircled by those strange hard children.

'Then I'll be one of them.'

They were right by her now. She looked up and through the mist glimpsed their legs and boots, their skirts and trews. They streamed past, hands linked, headlong as if downhill.

'Get her!'

'Catch her!'

She did not understand. They were gone now, their footsteps fading and their rough voices.

'Surely they saw me?'

Slowly she sat up. The mist had gone, and the peacock.

'They were after the other me!'

They were after the other Jessica, who had already half slipped out of the world, who was ripe to be caught.

'And if they catch her – what then? What would happen to *me*? Disappear? Would I disappear?'

All those other children had, those children from Welshpool over the centuries. But they had disappeared only from their own world. They still led a secret life here at Powis. In daylight they came only in a mist. She wondered whether night-time was their real play-time, when there were only the statues and the stars as witnesses.

She got to her feet and stood for a moment drawing in a deep breath, feeling herself at the centre of a spell.

'I'll do it!' she promised. 'I can.'

She was suddenly filled with a huge excitement. She repeated the words out loud.

'I'll do it. I promise!'

She stretched her arms wide, and heard the voices whispering, 'Jessica . . . Jessica . . . Jessica . . .'

The vow had been heard. It was sealed.

The first thing was to find Billy. Now, more than ever, he must be warned. The real Billy must surely be still in the real world, and unaware that he now had a danger-ous double.

'Can't be stonestruck already, else he'd have been in the chain with the others.'

She hoped this was true.

'He'll have gone back to Welshpool,' she decided.

He would have left the wide park with its terrifying deer for the more familiar territory of streets and houses.

There he could run free as he had in the streets of London, scavenging, taking his chances. She crossed the park for the third time that day, making for the high wrought-iron gates beyond the buttercup meadow and the lake.

When she reached the gate she found someone there. She heard the sobs first, and the sniffing. There, crouched by one of the stone posts, was that same small boy she had seen earlier.

'Trevor?'

He jumped as if stung. He had taken off his spectacles and blinked owlishly up at her, face wet and streaked.

'What's the matter?'

He shook his head and buried it again between his knees. Jessica stood helpless. The world seemed full of crying children. She sat beside him.

'Tell me,' she urged.

He lifted his head, rubbed his sleeve across his nose and put his glasses back on.

'You been – in there?' He jerked his head towards the park.

'Yes.'

He gazed fearfully at it, at the unimagined distances.

'Anyone see you?'

She shook her head, puzzled. He looked at her.

'Got to run off, see.'

'Why?'

'She'll kill me! Finks I did it.'

'Did what?'

'Punched 'er kid's nose and made it bleed. And I never, I never!'

His face began to crumple.

'So who did?'

'Dunno. Dunno 'is name. He was – he was at the pig bin – looking for food, I fink.'

'Billy!'

'And – and Jack saw 'im and started calling 'im names. Calls *me* names, 'n all. Calls me mucky vacky!'

'So the other boy hit him?'

'Yeah!' His face brightened at the memory. 'Didn't 'arf fetch 'im a wallop – wham!'

He punched the air with his own puny fist.

'Then ran off and left you to get the blame.'

He nodded, face pinched and scared again. He looked like a little old man.

'Can't never go back. She'll kill me. Hates me. But what'll I do! I ain't – I ain't got me gas mask!' His voice rose to a wail.

In London their gas masks went everywhere with them, in tins on straps they wore like satchels.

'You won't need it,' she told him. 'But, Trevor – you can't run off.'

If Trevor ran off to Powis he would disappear – he would disappear for ever, because he wanted to. She could not tell him that.

'Look, I'll go back with you and tell her it wasn't you.'

He looked at her, half hopeful, then shook his head.

'Won't believe you.'

'She will. I'll tell her I saw it – saw it with my own eyes.'

'But – that'd be calling Jack a liar!'

'So what? He is, isn't he? Come on.'

She stretched out a hand, and he took it. She helped him to his feet. He looked fearfully at the street ahead, hanging back. She began to walk.

'You know some girls called Gilly and Marlene?'

'Lived on our street. Woman they're wiv 'ates them, 'n all. They all do.'

'No they don't. You're just unlucky, that's all. The ones I'm with are nice.'

'You? A vacky?'

He did not believe it, any more than Billy had, or Marlene and Gilly.

'There he is!' a cry went up. 'Stinking vacky! Mam! Mam!'

The boy ran down a passage by the house. Trevor stopped and stiffened.

'That Jack?'

He nodded and gulped.

'Come on!'

When they reached the house there was no sign of Jack or his mother. Jessica boldly set off down the side passage. She could smell boiled cabbage and soapsuds. There was an outhouse, and through the open door she could see the tub and mangle. Trevor pulled at her sleeve.

'Sleep there,' he whispered.

'*What?*'

'Don't want fleas in the 'ouse.'

She peered round the door and saw, heaped on the stone floor, an untidy heap of blankets. She felt a huge rage, a helpless fury against the cruelty and unfairness of it all.

'So there you are!'

They both whirled round.

'And who're you, miss?'

'I've come to tell you what really happened. Trevor didn't hit Jack.'

91

'He did, he did, Mam!'

'Liar!' Jessica spat.

'Here, don't you go calling my –'

'I saw it!'

'I never saw you!'

'No, you didn't – too busy calling people names!'

'So who did then?' the woman demanded. 'Perhaps you'll tell me that, miss.'

'I – I don't know his name.'

'One of them mucky vackys, I'll be bound!'

'Yes. But it wasn't Trevor.' She looked straight at the woman. 'I'm Jessica Weaver. I'm staying with the Locketts up at the castle. They're really nice.'

It worked. The woman's expression changed.

'Oh. Stopping at the castle, is it. Know Rhoda well, I do. Posh girls' school there's meant to be coming.'

'Next week. I came early. My house was bombed. I'm an evacuee.'

She said the last words deliberately and almost proudly.

'Oh well.' The woman was nonplussed. Her eye fell on the cowering Trevor. 'Takes all sorts, I suppose.'

'Trevor and I are friends,' Jessica said. 'That's why I wanted you to know the truth.'

Again the woman looked at her. What Jessica was really saying was, 'Let me see you hit Trevor, and I'll go straight back to the castle and tell.'

'Jack!' The woman turned on her son. 'Is it?'

He was cornered.

'Why, you little –' She raised her hand, then remembered Jessica's presence and let it fall. Jack shrank back like one well used to warding off blows.

'She hits him,' Jessica thought, 'so I suppose he doesn't see why she shouldn't hit Trevor, too.'

She felt almost sorry for him.

'No one *wants* to be an evacuee,' she said. 'We don't like it any more than you do, Mrs . . .?'

'Evans.'

'You'll be all right now, Trevor.' She tugged her arm from his grasp. 'Goodbye, Mrs Evans.'

She kept walking, swiftly, half expecting Trevor to come after her. She did not really know whether she had done him any good. As soon as she had gone Mrs Evans could turn on him. Jack certainly would.

'Quite brave of me, really, sticking up for him like that.'

She was surprised at herself. She doubted whether she would have dared, a couple of days ago. That upsurge of courage she had felt when she made her vow seemed to be spilling over into real life.

'P'raps better *practise* being brave,' she thought.

She had owed Trevor something, anyway. He had seen what must, surely, be Billy, digging in the pig bins in the hope of finding something to eat. The Billy she had glimpsed earlier must have been his double. Now they were both in the same boat – the same danger.

The difference was that she knew. She knew that their shadow selves were playing a dangerous game of Chain Tag – of Fishes in a Net.

'But not stonestruck – not yet. And there must be a way to save us as well as him – Harry.'

There was a way. Lockett had spoken of a boy who had disappeared for days. He had come back to Welshpool babbling of peacocks and running chains of children. That boy would now be a man – as old as Lockett, or older, even. He could still be living here in Welshpool. It was an extraordinary thought.

'Can't exactly go knocking on doors, asking.'

That boy who had so nearly gone into the power of the Green Lady could now be butcher, baker, policeman – anything. But surely he would be marked out – it would show on his face. Surely he must even now have nightmares of pursuing children and treacherous peacocks? Or had he buried the memory, deep deep down, refused to think of it, just as she was refusing to think of . . .

'London Bridge is falling down falling down, falling
down
London Bridge is falling down, my fair lady . . .'

She did not hear or see the children till they were almost on her.

'Catch him!'

'Get him!'

She saw with horror a running chain of children. They rushed, swaying and pulling, between the grey houses, and ahead of them raced a small figure, legs going like pistons.

'Billy!' she screamed.

As he reached her she turned and ran with him, and he was running back the way she had come, back to the iron gates, back to the castle. He ran so fast that she could not keep up, the gap between them widened.

'Get *her*!' she heard the cry go up.

She sped between the iron gates and into the park. The cries and footsteps suddenly faded and died away. She looked swiftly over her shoulder, then halted. The children had dropped hands, were no longer a chain.

'Cheat!'

'Cowardy cowardy custard!'

These Welshpool children of today would not venture into the park. It was out of bounds – probably had been all their lives.

'We'll get you!'

'You wait!'

She turned away and saw that Billy had dropped to the ground, gasping for breath. She went and flopped beside him.

'I – was – looking for you!'

'Found me then, ain't yer?'

'To – warn you!'

'What about? Them deer ain't 'ere?'

He scanned nervously about.

'I told you – they won't hurt. But – but there's something else as well.'

'Thought you said there wasn't any tigers.'

'Oh, listen, will you! It's important.'

Then she told him. She told him everything – or at least, everything she knew.

Nine

'Two of me an' two of you?'

'Yes!'

'Garn!'

'No, it's true. You must believe me – it's dangerous.'

'Believe the other stuff. Ghosts 'n that. Pub on our corner's haunted.'

'Not exactly ghosts . . .'

'This 'orrible geezer with a bell.'

'What?'

'Lots of 'em've seen it. Ding dong ding dong, bring out yer dead!'

He mimicked in sepulchral tones.

'There was this plague, see, and you got this red patch and sneezed and then – pht! Dead. Snuffed it. It was because they was dirty in them days,' he added virtuously. 'Any case, knew this place was haunted.'

'How?'

''S arternoon. When you'd gone. Heard this 'orrible screech!'

He shuddered feelingly.

'The peacock!'

'Nah! Couldn't 've been a bird. Whistle, birds do.'

Jessica thought she knew what had happened. She

herself had heard that scream in the darkness on the night of her coming, when she had wished herself away. Billy, stricken with grief, had done the same. And his wishing self had slipped silently and invisibly away, marked only by the peacock's screech.

'You'll soon know,' she told him.

'Know what?'

'You'll *see* the peacock. You'll see everything, before too long.'

He eyed her suspiciously.

'This ain't a daft game, is it?'

'No – it's serious. Dead serious.'

'Come on then, let's see 'em!' He marched off, forgetting the deer. 'Watch out, spookies, 'ere we come.'

Jessica hurried after him.

'Wheee, spooks . . . wheee!'

'Billy, it's not like that!'

He stopped so suddenly that she banged right into him.

'Here! It's day! Come out at night, spooks do!'

'I keep telling you, it's not like that. It's real, and . . . and . . .' She hardly knew how to say it. 'Billy, this is really important. Mind what you wish!'

He stared.

'You what?'

'Mind what you wish. You've already wished yourself away once – must've done, or you wouldn't have a double.'

'Wish meself away! Don't I just! I wish –'

'No!'

'You're barmy, vacky!'

'No! Please, Billy, please!'

He shrugged.

'No skin off my nose!' He carried on, walking now, kicking with his boots. 'Any rate, never wished out loud. Nobody 'eard.'

'It doesn't make any difference. A wish is a wish whether you say it or not.'

They carried on a little way in silence.

'Billy . . . did you get anything to eat?'

'Ooh yes, lovely grub! Bits of raw carrots and spuds! Feel like a bleeding rabbit!'

'The Green Lady . . . that old woman, Priscilla. She puts out food. Bread and apples.'

'Oooh, don't!' He groaned and clutched his stomach.

'But you're not to eat it.'

'Why?'

'Because . . . because . . .' She was only guessing, but certain she was right. 'If you do, I think it'll give her power over you. She tried to make me take an apple.'

'Ooh, apples!'

'I'll bring you food. I promise.'

They were in the gardens now. He sat on a step and fished in his torn pockets.

'Could swap this, I s'pose.'

She recognized the grey twisted metal. Most of the kids had a hoard of shrapnel. They searched the gutters for it after every raid, like beachcombers after a high tide. It was the visible harvest of war.

'Bet the kids round here've never seen any.'

'Bet they haven't,' she agreed.

'Bet I could swap that,' he held up a large jag of metal, 'for a cake. A whole cake. A choc'late cake.'

'Bet you could. But save it – for emergencies. I'll get you some food.'

'What – now?'

'Yes. Mrs Lockett's always baking.'

She hesitated. To go back to the castle was to go to a world where telephones rang, where terrible messages came.

'Go on, then!'

'Billy . . .'

'What?'

But she could not bring herself to tell him. When things are said they are made real, part of the real world.

'Nothing.'

'Go on then! Cor, vacky, 'ave a heart! I'm starving!'

She went. After a few paces she turned.

'Don't eat anything while I'm gone, and – watch it!'

She went on her way.

'Watch it yerself, vacky!'

Mrs Lockett was laying the table for tea. There was a warm scent of newly baked scones.

'Ah, there you are, dearie.'

'Never called me that before,' Jessica thought. 'Sorry for me. So it is true.'

'Had a nice time, did you? I've baked some lovely scones and look – ham sandwiches. There's a treat.'

'Lovely.' She thought fast. 'But – what I came to ask you . . .'

'What's that, dear?'

'A picnic! I thought I'd like a picnic!'

Mrs Lockett looked startled.

'It's just that – well, in London we haven't got a garden, and I just thought it'd be fun.'

'Well, dear, it's years since I –'

'Oh, I didn't mean you! Just me! I know a place where I could have it. Please!'

'Funny old idea that is, picnicking by yourself.'

'Please!'

And so a basket was packed.

'I'm ever so hungry,' Jessica said. 'Must be the fresh air.'

'That'll be it. Nothing like country air and food to build you up.'

'Unless you're Billy,' Jessica thought, 'or Trevor, and Marlene and Gilly.'

Jessica found Billy where she had left him. He was brave enough on the streets, but this was a foreign country, a jungle.

'Cor, lovely grub!'

He fell on the basket wolfishly, pulling out sandwiches, one in each hand, cramming his mouth.

'You're supposed to chew before you swallow.'

She took a sandwich and nibbled it, watching him. She had been hungry herself, but never like this.

'You'll bust,' she told him.

He did not answer, having polished off the sandwiches and started on the scones. He seemed not even to see her, let alone hear, his whole being concentrated on the food. Only after the second scone did he pause for a breath.

'Phew!' He patted his belly, gazed at the remaining food and swiftly stowed it into his pockets, scones, boiled eggs, apples and all. 'That's better!'

'There's butter and jam in those scones,' she told him. 'You'll ruin your jacket.'

'Ham!' he said lovingly. 'Never 'ardly gets ham, 'cept at Christmas.'

'Same here. Corned beef. Spam.'

'You get grub like this every day?'

'Sort of.'

'Cor! Wish I lived 'ere!' He gazed longingly up at the sun-washed pink of the castle.

'Don't!'

'What?'

'Wish. I told you!'

'Temper temper, vacky!'

'It's dangerous. I keep telling you.'

'Pah!' He stuck his thumb on his nose and wagged his finger. The food had restored him to his old self.

'What'll you do tonight?' she asked. She already had a plan.

'Dunno.'

'Would you dare . . . would you dare sleep here?'

'Ain't frit. Ain't frit of nuffin'.'

'I know. I know you're not. It's just that I wondered . . .'

She wondered what happened in Powis at night. She wondered whether those rough children ran visible in the moonlight, whether the spell deepened? Or perhaps there was something she did not yet know, a secret beyond secrets.

'I will if you will,' she said.

'Will what, vacky?'

'I don't *mind* you calling me that, so you needn't keep doing it!'

'What, vacky?'

He grinned. Then, seeing something beyond her, he sprang to his feet and was gone. She turned and saw Lockett climbing steadily up to the castle.

Hastily she tidied the plundered basket, tried to look like someone who had just quietly picnicked on her own.

'Hello, Lockett.'

He paused, breathing hard.

'Gets steeper, that climb.'

'I've been having a picnic. Mrs Lockett said I could.'

'That's nice, then. Good as a feast.'

'Yes.' She wondered whether he knew about the telephone call, the terrible news.

'Give you plenty, did she?'

'Oh yes – yes.'

'That's right. Plenty to eat, war or no war. No need to go getting it anywhere else.'

She stared up at him. He knew! He knew about the little larders of bread and apples. He was warning her.

'I know,' she said. 'I do know.'

'Good. Good, then.'

He looked up at the castle.

'Sometimes you have to do a hard thing.'

He spoke as if to himself, as if he were thinking aloud.

'What?'

But he shook his head and carried on, slow and sure. He was hardly out of sight when Billy reappeared.

'Who's that old geezer?'

'Lockett. It's them I'm stopping with.'

'Where's 'is crown, then?' He pranced, making mock bows. 'Arternoon, yer majesty! Yes, yer royal 'ighness, no, yer royal 'ighness, three bags full, yer royal 'ighness!'

'Idiot!' she told him. 'Listen, about tonight . . .'

She told him her plan. She knew, even as she did so, that it was only partly because there might be other clues she could snatch out of the darkness. It was also because she wanted Billy to see with his own eyes that chain of children, perhaps even that pale, riding boy.

He had heard the peacock scream. She wanted him to see that glossy head and gorgeous fan. The burden of secrets was too heavy for her to bear alone.

'I will if you will,' she finished cunningly.

'They won't let you.'

'They won't know. I'll wait till they've gone to bed, then come.'

He surveyed her suspiciously.

'How do I know you would? Chicken out, you could.'

'I won't – I swear it!'

'Cross yer 'eart and hope to die?'

'Yes.'

'Say it.'

'Cross my heart and hope to die.'

'Bright out, last night.'

'I know.'

'Blooming great moon. Proper good night for Jerry!'

In London they'd prayed for cloud at the full moon. When the sky was clear the whole city lay bathed in light, a perfect target, blackout or no blackout.

'There isn't any Jerry here.'

'Nah. Just ghosties – sez you!'

'You'll be able to see for yourself. Will you or won't you?'

He hesitated and looked nervously about. He had seen no peacock, no running chain of children. It was the space that frightened him.

'You could stop in the orangery till I come – where you were that day in the rain.'

He delved again in the basket, found the pop bottle and unplugged it.

'Will you?'

He put the bottle to his lips and tilted back his head. Glug glug glug, on and on. Then, gasping and in a spray of fizz, 'Yeah!'

It was decided. They would explore the night together.

'You wait in the orangery till I come.'

''Less I see sumfink.'

'Whatever you see, don't go out!'

'Shall if I want!'

'No! No. You still don't realize, do you?'

'Fink you know everyfing, don't yer! Lah di dah di dah!'

'Oh, *you*!'

She seized the bottle herself then and tilted it, but the fizz went straight up her nose and she choked, eyes gushing. The bottle was tugged from her grasp. Billy took the tumbler from the basket and poured the pop. He held it out to her, grinning.

'Here yer go, ducks. Drink it proper. Ladylike.'

'What – like champagne?'

She took the glass, daintily curving her little finger. She sipped delicately.

'Delicious!'

'A toast!'

He jumped up and raised the bottle.

'The King, God bless 'im!'

'The King!'

One sipped, the other glugged.

'Anuvver! The Green Woman!'

She spluttered again.

'No! Lady, anyway, Green Lady. Not her!'

'Right then – vackys – vackys everywhere!'

'Vackys everywhere!'

They drank the toast. All about them the birds whistled and the garden breathed in all its secret places, and invisible ears, perhaps, listened.

Ten

J essica stepped out of the castle and into the full light
of the moon. The world lay hushed and flooded by
its cold brilliance. She went softly, aware of her own
footsteps on stone. The shadows were black and deep
enough to swallow you. She began to wonder how
many lonely paces she must make before she reached
the orangery and Billy.

She turned into the narrow winding path that
led to the pool in one direction, the terraces in
the other. Now she was off home ground. She was
walking away from safety and into the spellbound
valley.

'All you have to remember is not to wish,' she told
herself, but only half believed it. Above her the leaden
figures danced and piped against the sky, silvered and
silent. All the daytime green was bleached. The gardens
were re-made and strange.

With relief she saw ahead the glass of the orangery,
struck by white fire. Behind it, Billy would be waiting.
There would be two of them against whatever terrors
the night held.

A door stood ajar. She peered in. From the shadows
stared the blank eyes of the disembodied white heads.

There was a deep stone silence. Impossible to imagine a warm, breathing human presence.

'Billy!' she whispered, clutched by panic. 'Billy!'

Slowly she stepped forward, looking about. Then she saw him, curled as he had been when she first found him there, asleep.

'The beast!' She was filled with indignation. While she had been making that fearful journey he had been calmly sleeping, not even keeping watch. She shook him roughly.

'Billy!'

He shot up.

'What? Where? Oh!'

''S me, you idiot! Wake up!'

'Am awake, ain't I?' he said bitterly. He rubbed his eyes. 'What d'you do that for!'

He dropped back again and shut his eyes.

'Wake *up*!'

'Don't want to,' he mumbled. 'Leave me alone.'

He curled an arm across his eyes to shut off her and the moonlight.

'You pig, you pig!' She pummelled his shoulder. He wriggled and grunted.

'Get up!' She seized an arm with both hands and pulled. He tugged it away.

'All right, all *right*!'

Then he was sitting up and properly awake.

'Must be barmy! Middle of the night!'

'Come on!' She pulled him to his feet. 'The peacock, remember, and the children!'

They stepped from the orangery on to the terrace, where the jacket of the solitary piper lifted in the windless air.

Billy was silent. She turned and saw that his eyes had gone to silver and were staring out over the vast, moon-washed valley. The silence was enormous. It was as if they were encountering night for the first time – real night.

Something was going to happen. The hush was expectant, a holding of the breath. Jessica felt the hairs stir at the nape of her neck.

> 'Girls and boys come out to play
> The moon doth shine as bright as day . . .'

It was a child's voice, thin and sweet. Billy clutched at her sleeve.

> 'Leave your supper and leave your treats
> And join your playfellows in the streets.'

'Whassat?' His voice was a hoarse whisper.
'Ssshh!'
The voice seemed to come not from the gardens, but from above. She turned and craned back upwards at the rearing wall of the castle with its blank windows.

> 'Come with a whoop and come with a call
> And come with a goodwill or not at all . . .'

Now Billy, too, had turned and was staring upwards. The singing stopped.

Then, from high up something came drifting down. It fluttered like a leaf, wove its way down the shafting moonlight, gleaming pale. They gazed up, rapt and transfixed. And as they did so they saw another whitish gleam, and another. They fell in eerie and silent procession, messages from nowhere, from another world.

The first glided before them to the frosted stone of the terrace. Jessica moved dumbly forward and as she stooped another curved past and almost grazed her face.

She picked up the paper – parchment – oddly stiff between her fingers. In the piercing light she saw the spidery words, and shivered, because she knew they were meant for her.

'What's it say?'

Billy whispered by her ear. He bent and snatched up another scrap. And then a third sailed by and it drifted outwards, over the greenish silver balustrade, and they watched as it went down, down, into the darkness and out of reach.

'Quick!'

Jessica ran and as she did so another paper sailed by and she plucked it out of the air, chill and frail. Along the terrace and down the stone steps she fled, fixed on the strange moonlit paperchase.

Once on the lower path she looked upwards to mark the solitary leaden figure.

'Here!' she whispered. 'Somewhere here!'

There was no sign of it on the path, and so she stepped into the wide bed and pulled at the shrubs so that they went into silvery shivers and made little hissing whispers of protest.

'Must be somewhere!'

Billy had already given up. He was back on the path, squinting down at his own two scraps of paper. Suddenly she too was seized with the desire to know what messages had been dropped forlornly from that high tower into the night. She peered down at the first parchment.

'Here I write from this cold manor . . .' she read.

Then Billy:

'Have pity on me . . .'

They stared at one another. Jessica looked at her second scrap.

'Long away from the world in this high room . . .'

'There's another,' Billy said, and read, 'Save me and save my brother . . .'

Awestruck, Jessica raised her eyes to the sheer walls of the castle. She thought she glimpsed a tiny movement high up, a hand, perhaps, waving. In that instant the whispering began.

'Jessica . . . Jessica . . . Jessica . . .'

The air was crowded with her name, soft and insistent. She wheeled about and saw no one but Billy, still poring over the parchments.

'Jessica . . . Jessica . . . Jessica . . .'

She put her hands over her ears to shut out the clamour and saw that Billy was looking at her, puzzled and half fearful. A horrid thought struck her.

'Can't you hear it?' He shook his head. 'The whispering! My name!'

He could not. He evidently believed her, though, because he looked fearfully about him.

Then the peacock screamed. They froze, both of them, made statues momentarily by the shock.

A moment ago the peacock had not been there. Now he was, and he too had silver eyes, and all his gaudy colours were ashen and blackened as if he had walked through fire.

Jessica heard Billy's whispered 'Cor!' and felt him clutch at her arm.

110

The peacock gazed at them and they at him, an awkward triangle under the moon. They stood locked for what seemed a long time.

Then the peacock turned and trod away and the pair, entranced, went after him. They did not know where he would lead them and they did not speak, their eyes fixed on his gleaming crown.

He halted. Jessica looked beyond him and saw herself and Billy reflected. The two figures stood pallid and insubstantial, their eyes cavernous. She felt Billy's grip tighten.

'It's us!'

He made as if to turn and bolt but she held him fast. That other pair who stood watching were strangely adrift, unrooted. Jessica looked down and saw her own shadow, knife-edge clear, and Billy's. She looked again at the others and saw that they stood in uninterrupted moonlight.

'It's us!' came Billy's hoarse whisper again.

'No – look! No shadows!'

Then the Green Lady was there. She made herself out of the smoky light.

'Jessica!' she said softly, and that other Jessica turned her head. The Green Lady smiled and beckoned, and the other Jessica smiled and took a step towards her. Then another step.

'No!' screamed Jessica. 'No!'

The shadow self leapt back and the Green Lady's narrow face twisted.

'Beware!' she cried, and as she dissolved there came the distant drumming of feet, the calls and yells as the stonestruck children came.

Jessica flattened herself against the wall and pulled Billy after her, but their doubles stood blank and motionless. The human chain advanced. A few seconds more and that helpless pair would be encircled, trapped – fishes in a net.

'Run!' she screamed. 'Oh, quick – run!'

'Run for it!' Billy bawled.

Their doubles hesitated for an instant, then turned and fled. They flickered among the trees and vanished.

Jessica turned and for the first time saw the children plain, and saw that they were all grey, like stone. It was as if a string of statues had come to life.

The leader halted and the rest behind him. She heard their panting, their rasping breath.

'Where are they?'

'Catch 'em!'

'Sshh! Watch!'

They all stood and they all looked for their quarry, and their eyes glittered in their grey faces. Eyes, nose, mouth all grey.

Jessica felt their menace and flattened herself against the wall, scarcely breathing. The battery of cold eyes raked the deserted gardens. They stayed poised so long that it was as if time, too, had turned to stone.

Then one of them dropped his hand from the link and pointed.

'There!'

The grey heads turned to follow the pointing finger. They tilted upwards and the moon shone full on those mask faces.

'After 'em!'

The leader raised an arm and began to run, and 'Catch a fish!' 'Catch a fish!' – the hiss went down the chain as it moved after him, gathering speed.

It curved out of sight, but still Jessica and Billy

stayed motionless, listening. It was their own selves who were being pursued, their careless wishing selves, half-way to being stonestruck.

'Wish for them not to be caught!' Jessica whispered suddenly.

'What?'

'Go on. Wish for it! Do it!'

She screwed her own eyes tight and wished for the escape of that other Jessica and that other Billy. It was a wish strong enough to be a prayer. At last the drumming feet faded. She opened her eyes.

'Safe!'

'What?'

'Must be. Or we wouldn't still be here.'

'Did you see 'em? Grey they was – all grey! 'Orrible!' He shuddered.

'Stonestruck.'

'What if they got *us*?'

'It's us they're *after*!'

'Ooh, that was 'orrible, 'n all! You and me – plain as the nose on yer face! 'Ow did we get there?'

'I told you. Wishing. Now do you believe me?'

'Was that 'er? That woman?'

'The Green Lady. Yes.'

'Now what? Ain't stopping 'ere – no fear!'

She looked at him. He was braver than she was, she knew. But he dared not stay out here where those grey children were on the loose.

'I'll stop with you. We'll go back to the orangery and sleep there.'

She would have to hope that she woke up in time to return to the castle before she was missed. There was nothing else she could do.

'Fanks, vacky!'

They stepped away from the sheltering wall, still cautious, still listening. Jessica saw that she was holding the pieces of parchment, and remembered with a shock the singing voice.

'Here – 'ave mine. I don't want 'em.'

Billy thrust his own scraps into her hand. The words were stark in the moonlight.

'Have pity on me . . .' she said softly. Again she raised her eyes to the castle walls for a sign. They rose vast and blank, their daytime rose gone to night-time grey.

'The other piece!' She remembered that they had been searching when the peacock screamed.

'Leave it! 'Ow do we know they won't come back! Come on!'

'No! I must find it!'

She took a step forward and saw it, caught on a leafy plant like an unlikely flower.

'Here!'

She took it up. There was only one word scrawled in that childish hand.

'Jessica.'

Eleven

I n the end Jessica decided to leave Billy sleeping. She looked down on him, peaceful as he never was waking.

'At least asleep he's safe and not wishing.'

She went out of the orangery and shivered. The sun was cold. She remembered the colder shining of the night, and shivered again at the memory of that singing voice, those grey-faced children. She could see again those slowly drifting parchments, those shadowless doubles, and because she was seeing them instead of the world about her she did not see Lockett until it was too late. Hastily she brushed her dusty coat, arranged her face.

'Jessica? Up in the morning early, is it?'

'I – I couldn't sleep.' He was watching her closely. She had a sudden inspiration. 'I – the castle isn't haunted, is it?'

'Haunted?'

'I – in the night I thought I heard singing. A child.'

'Ah.'

'I really did hear it! And I wondered . . . is it part of the story?'

'They shut her up . . .' he murmured.

'What?'

'His sister. After he'd been taken by the Green Lady. To keep her safe.'

Save me and save my brother. The words were in her pocket.

'Up in a high room, they say. And I'll tell you this.'

She waited.

'There's no one knows the number of rooms in that castle. Not exact.'

'*What?*'

'What they say.'

'Like the children!'

He looked at her.

'Never count children twice – never!'

'Aye, like that, I suppose.'

'But all they've got to do is count the number of doors!'

'Oh yes,' he agreed. 'That's all. But it depends, see.'

'On what?'

'On who's doing the counting.'

There was a long silence.

'Lockett . . .?' She hesitated, not knowing how to put it into words. 'If you see anything – children, say – you won't say anything, will you?' She did not mean those others, she meant Billy, Trevor even.

He smiled then.

'Not a word. Learned that years ago, I did. Oh yes . . .' He seemed suddenly far away. 'Learned that, I did, early on, to keep a secret. Safest thing, that is.'

'Safe?'

He came back to himself.

'You be careful, Jessica,' he said. 'Welshpool, this is, not London.'

'Children go missing, you mean.'

'Something like that.'

'But one came back, you said so.'

'Long time ago, that was.'

'*You* remember it.'

'Ah, well. Only just.'

He had started on towards his garden. He did not want to talk about it.

She had hoped to coax out of him a name, someone she might perhaps have visited, asked questions – if she dared. Oddly, she thought perhaps she might have dared. Since that moment when she had vowed to save Harry she had found herself much braver than she could have imagined. It was as if she was drawing courage from the vow itself.

It was easy enough to reach her room without meeting Mrs Lockett. She spent the time till breakfast writing her story. Now and then her eye fell on the scraps of parchment lying on the bed beside her.

Here I write from this cold manor.

Have pity on me.

Long away from the world in this high room.

Save me and save my brother.

Jessica.

Somewhere in Powis was a child entombed in loneliness, a girl in a high room level with the sky. She was imprisoned as surely as her brother under the Green Lady's spell.

'Better if they'd let her out, and the Green Lady had taken her, too,' she thought. 'At least they'd have had one another.'

She knew what she must do that day.

'Once I've taken Billy some food, I'll do it.'

She would comb that huge castle and try its doors one by one. If there was a missing room, she would find it. Her name was written on the parchment. She had been chosen.

When she had finished writing she laid the parchments carefully between the pages of the book and closed it. She sat staring ahead at the photographs on the chest of drawers.

'Oh, Dad . . .'

But even as she gazed a thought struck her, and she gasped with shock.

'Mum!'

That phone call – she did not know who had been at the other end of the line! At the time she had supposed it was her mother, but what if . . .? What if it had been some unknown official voice, and the bad news had been not about her father, but her mother? Images of newsreels flashed in her head, of marching soldiers, wounded soldiers, ambulances. She heard the ratatat of gunfire, the whine of shells.

Then she remembered the coldness of her parting from her mother, her own stony muteness, broken only by those fierce words, 'What about me, what about *me*?'

She heard her name called. Here, in the huge slow peace of Powis, while hundreds of miles away the war went on, breakfast was ready.

Afterwards it was easy enough to assemble a breakfast of sorts for Billy – bread, ham, a handful of biscuits. She slipped out and hurried through the garden.

'It's like having a pet to feed,' she thought, and then wished she hadn't, because she remembered Henry, and he, too, had gone missing. She conjured him up as he was when he visited her in bed, loud growling purr and paws urgently treading the eiderdown.

'No one to feed him now, even if he is still alive. And no warm patch by the stairs.'

When Jessica reached the orangery and found Billy gone it was as if she had half expected it. She was becoming used to living in a world of uncertainties. She stood staring at the spot where he had lain, then turned.

'I don't suppose you know where he's gone,' she told the sternly gazing white men. 'You should've kept a better eye on him!'

She would hide the food and come back later, when she had done what she had to do in the castle. She stooped to place it among the rubbery foliage.

'Oh, he won't be needing that.' The soft voice of the old woman, Priscilla.

Jessica turned. There she stood, basket on arm, smiling.

'That little lad'll not go hungry,' she said. 'Not with me to tend him.'

Jessica stared, horrified, into those cunning eyes. She had warned him, had thought he had understood. Could he really have taken bread, fruit from this dangerous old woman?

'There's always mouths to feed at Powis,' said Priscilla. 'Always children coming and going.' She took an apple from the basket. 'Have it. There's plenty and to spare.'

Dumbly Jessica shook her head.

'The children are always hungry. They run and run all night.'

'I know,' said Jessica, and looked straight into her

eyes with her new-found courage. 'And I know who you are!'

The creature stiffened.

'What?' she hissed.

'I know who you are,' Jessica repeated. 'And I'll never take anything from you, never!'

It was as if her own words were a spell. Priscilla gave a scream of rage and drew herself up in her dingy rags. Then, impossibly, there sprang around her a green fire; spears of green flame leapt up and Priscilla was there shimmering behind them, and she screamed one last word: 'Beware!' The emerald flames licked and roared. Slowly she melted, dissolved into them and was gone.

Jessica stared at the spot where fire had been only seconds before. She was terrified and triumphant. What she had witnessed was proof of the Green Lady's power. But now she knew that she too had power, of a sort.

She edged carefully round the place where the fire had been, out into the fresh morning, then ran. She ran back to the castle, back to a world of ordinariness, where clocks ticked and breakfast things still lay on the table.

'Ah, there you are, Jessica.' Mrs Lockett had washed the breakfast things and taken off her pinafore. 'I was coming to look for you.'

She was going into Welshpool, wanted Jessica to help carry the shopping.

'Can't ask Lockett every time. Got to save petrol, see.'

Jessica's search for the missing room would have to wait. She was half glad, still dazed by that green fire. Billy was probably already in Welshpool searching the pig bins or bartering for food with his hoard of shrapnel.

'That's if he isn't already stonestruck.'

She had pushed the thought away for as long as she could, but now it surfaced. She could not know for certain whether Priscilla had been telling the truth when she said Billy had taken food from her. She would not know for certain until – or if – she found him.

'If she's got him, it'll be me on my own again. Just me against her!'

She would be alone in a world of screaming peacocks, grey-faced children and green devouring fire.

In Welshpool smells of cooking wafted, cars and bicycles went by and the sounds of Welsh and London voices filled the streets.

'I shall do the shopping, then go and have a bit of a sit down at Megan's,' Mrs Lockett said. 'Give you a chance to look round, it will.'

Jessica was already looking round. She was looking for Billy, Trevor, Marlene and Gilly – for any familiar face.

It was not until the shopping was done and they were making their way back that she spotted them.

'Oh, thank goodness – Billy!'

He was squatting on the pavement, and with him were Marlene and Gilly.

'I – I think I'll just go and have a look round,' she said.

'Give me the basket then, dear. And you come to Megan's in a bit – know where it is, do you? Right next the Post Office.'

Jessica flew towards the huddle in the gutter.

'Hello!'

They all looked up at her with their sharp, grubby faces.

'Why did you go? I brought you breakfast, I said I would!'

'Marlene and Gilly's stopping with a witch!'

'Is it true?' asked Gilly. 'About that castle place?'

'Is what true?'

'Told 'em,' Billy said.

'Oh, Billy!' He had been boasting, showing off.

'Don't matter.'

'Don't believe it, anyhow,' Marlene said. 'Load of old tripe.'

'But is it true there's two of 'im and two of you?' Gilly was round-eyed, awestruck.

'Yes, it is.' She admitted it reluctantly.

'Garn!' remarked Marlene. 'He's a liar.'

'And there's this great big bird wiv a long tail,' Gilly said. '*I* want to see it.'

'Well, you can't,' Marlene told her. 'Cos there ain't one, see.'

Billy shrugged.

'No skin off my nose,' he said. 'Least I ain't stopping with a witch. Least I ain't stopping with anyone. Least I ain't got fleas.'

Marlene gave him a shove and he fell sideways into the gutter.

'You say that again and I'll black yer eye!' she told him. Then, to Jessica, 'He up at that palace place wiv you?'

'Sort of,' said Jessica cautiously.

'No I ain't then! Told you – I ain't stopping anywhere!'

'It's not fair!' wailed Gilly. '*I* don't want to stop anywhere! I want to go 'ome!'

'Well, you can't, so shut it!' Marlene told her.

'When can I then?'

'Soon,' said Marlene. 'Don't expect wars last long.'

'Tomorrow?'

'Oh, don't be daft!'

'Next week, then?'

'P'raps.'

'This year next year sometime never,' said Billy unhelpfully.

Gilly began to wail.

'It's not never, is it? It's not never!'

'Course it ain't!' Marlene glared at Billy. 'You keep out of it! Everyone knows you're a liar, Billy Turnbull!'

She looked sourly at Jessica.

'What d'you keep hanging round for? Come on, Gilly!' She pulled her sister to her feet. 'Staring!'

'I want to see that big bird! I want –'

'Come *on*!'

The pair went off, one dragging the other.

'Good riddance,' said Billy.

'You shouldn't have told them. It's a secret.'

'Oh, lah di dah! Keep your knickers on.'

'And if you keep coming to Welshpool you'll get found out, and they'll make you stay with someone.'

'Have to catch me first.'

'I brought you breakfast.'

'Fanks.'

'So are you coming back?'

He was screwing up his eyes, looking beyond her.

'There's that kid again!'

Jessica turned. She too recognized that small figure making its way uncertainly towards them.

'Run!'

'*What?*'

'He might ask where you're stopping! He's staying with someone Mrs Lockett knows.'

'So what?'

'He could *tell* her, idiot! Do you want to stop on the run, or not?'

She knew that she wanted him to. He was her only ally.

'Oh well.' He got up with exaggerated carelessness. 'Just going anyhow. Got fings to do.'

He sauntered off, hands in pockets.

'See you later!' she called after him. 'Got something to tell you!'

He did not reply. She sighed. Billy was almost as unpredictable as the peacock himself, as the stonestruck children.

Trevor came slowly, eyes downcast, as if not looking at the world made him invisible. He seemed to have shrunk since Jessica had last seen him, trousers flapping loosely over the matchstick legs. The legs, ending in knobbly boots, reminded her of the posters for Cherry Blossom boot polish.

'Hello.'

He looked up but did not smile. She could not imagine him smiling.

''Lo.'

'You all right?'

'Yeah.'

'That Jack's not been hitting you again?'

He shook his head. She did not know whether to believe him. He was like a little drooping bird.

'Wish I was 'ome,' he said miserably.

There it was again, another wish. Welshpool was full, fuller than it had ever been, of children who wished themselves away. And only she knew the danger.

'My ma wouldn't 've sent me if she'd known.'

'It's safer here.'

'I ain't scared of bombs. Look!' He lowered his voice and looked round. He pulled a crumpled envelope from his pocket.

'I've wrote Ma a letter!'

Jessica realized with a pang that she could not write to her own mother. She no longer had an address to write to.

'Asked her to come and fetch me! She could – she could come on the train and fetch me! She give me this envelope, see, wiv a stamp 'n all. Said I was to write and tell 'er how I was getting on.'

'Does Mrs Evans know?'

'Course not! She'd kill me!'

'Vacky, vacky, mucky vacky!'

They saw him too late. Trevor gasped and tried to hide the letter but Jack snatched it and held it high above his head.

'Mammy's boy's been writing home! What's he put?'

Jack danced back a few paces and tore the envelope open.

'No! No!'

'Give it back!' Jessica went towards him but he ran off a way then turned.

'Tell-tale tit, your tongue shall split! You keep your nose out, lah di dah!'

He raced off. She turned. Trevor was still standing there, tears rolling down his face. She did not know what to say. Jack would read the letter and then, as likely as not, show it to his mother.

Trevor, she found herself thinking, would almost be better off stonestruck.

Twelve

'**I** 've thought of something to do this afternoon.'
'What's that, dear?' Mrs Lockett was spooning out custard, deliciously scented. She called Jessica 'dear' nearly all the time now.

'I thought it'd be fun to explore.'

'That's nice, dear. Not by the lake, though.'

'Inside, I mean. The castle.'

'But I showed you, the other day.'

'No, I mean by myself. It'd be exciting. Pretend I'm the prince out of Sleeping Beauty and the castle's been enchanted for a hundred years.'

'It's ever so big . . . Lord knows how many rooms.'

That was exactly the point. No one did know exactly how many rooms. And in one, uncounted room sat a solitary child who had been waiting longer than a hundred years.

'Told the men, I did, when they came.'

'What men?'

'What? Oh, from the Ministry, I expect. When they came about your school. Be here in a day or two, I expect.'

'Who will?'

'Bringing beds, they said. Use the biggest rooms for

dormitories, see. Got to get a move on. I expect you're looking forward to seeing all your friends again.'

'Oh, I am!' Jessica had given her schoolfriends hardly a thought. They belonged in another world. The very thought of them bursting into this quiet valley was astonishing. The minute they arrived things would change. There would be no time for secret meetings, for following a peacock, unravelling threads. Perhaps the whole story would stop in its tracks, the pale boy and the stonestruck children dissolve into some green limbo out of time, waiting for the silence to return. Time was running out.

'Are any of the rooms locked?'

'Oh, they've all got locks, of course, had to have, in those days.'

The girl who had dropped those parchments into the night air had been put in that high stone room and the key turned in the lock. Then the days had started to run, the weeks, months, years, centuries.

'Just look at the size of some of them!'

Mrs Lockett had opened a cupboard and there, in bunches and hanging on nails, were the keys. There seemed hundreds of them.

'Got tags, see, most of them. But there's some I've never used. No point in your taking them, dear.'

'But couldn't I just –'

'There's none of the rooms locked.'

'Except one,' Jessica thought.

'You mustn't touch anything, mind. Not that you would, I know that, dear. Not like those little gutter-snipes in Welshpool.'

'Why don't you like them?' Jessica asked, suddenly furious. 'Why does nobody like them?'

Mrs Lockett looked startled.

'Oh, I don't think –'

'They can't help being here. They don't want to be.'

'Oh, I'm sure they're – it's just – outsiders, see.'

'Can you remember being a child?'

Mrs Lockett stared, shook her head.

'The world's for grown-ups, not children! They can do anything. Post you off somewhere like a parcel then forget all about you!'

'Oh dear!'

'And round here's worse than anywhere. Children disappearing! Did you count the children off that train? Did you? How d'you know one hasn't disappeared already?'

'Oh, I'm sure –'

'So why didn't you count them? Why did you throw that list away – I saw you!'

Jessica made for the door, then turned.

'*I* might disappear!' she said, and ran.

She heard Mrs Lockett calling after her but she ran, making for the deep cold heart of the castle.

She went first through the huge, grand rooms with their ghostly drapes, rooms where life had come to a halt when the war started. But she was looking for another, smaller room, where life had stopped centuries ago, when a lordling called Harry had been taken by the Green Lady.

She tried the handle of the first closed door she came to. Slowly it swung open. The room was bare but for a pile of broken chairs. She ran to the window and looked out. Below was the winding drive that led to the meadows and the iron gate to Welshpool. Deer were grazing, heads bent, marvellously separate and self-contained.

She was on the wrong side of the castle. Somehow she must work her way round. She left the wide landing behind to follow a narrow stone passage. And then the whispering began.

'Jessica . . . Jessica . . . Jessica . . .'

This whispering came not from a chain of stone-struck children but one solitary child. And it did not come hissing from spiteful tongues, but slowly, hesitantly, as if the name were being tried out for the first time.

'Jessica . . . Jessica . . .'

'I'm coming,' she whispered back. 'I'm trying to find you!'

She opened door after door. They swung open to reveal rooms small and large, all dusty, all half empty. Some were lit by high, narrow windows, and others were windowless, like cells. They were all little pockets of stopped time.

'Jessica . . . Jessica . . . Jessica . . .'

The whisper ran along the stone passage but she could not tell where it was coming from. It seemed before, behind and above her as if it were part of the air.

She was running again. She flung open doors, saw beyond, then pulled them shut again. Again and again she repeated the actions until she was half dizzy. Open shut run, open shut run. Then . . .

The door did not budge. She had turned the heavy iron ring and pushed. She tried again, this time pushing with her shoulder in case the door was stuck.

The whispering stopped, leaving a huge silence. In that silence she heard a child's voice.

'Jessica?'

She heard it plain, her name spoken with that questioning, half disbelieving inflection.

'Yes! It's me – Jessica! Are you there?'

She tried the door again, desperately.

'Here I write from this cold manor.'

'Don't be scared! There's no one here, only me.'

No reply.

'I got your messages.'

She put her ear to the door.

'Have pity on me.'

Those words, scrawled on a scrap of parchment.

'Long away from the world in this high room.'

The voice was soft and murmuring, the voice of one speaking as she writes.

'Save me and save my brother.'

'I will! I will! I'm here!' Jessica beat on the door with her fists. 'Come to the door and talk to me!'

Silence.

'Are you there?'

That same dense silence, absolute absence of sound. Even the whispers fled.

'Listen, I'll get the key!' She repeated the words very clearly and distinctly. 'I'll get the key and I'll come back!'

She waited, but knew there would be no reply. It was as if in the last few moments she had tapped into another time, another dimension, even. Those same bleak words that had drifted through the moonlight had been imprinted on the air as if on wax. What she had heard had been words played back as if on a gramophone record. There was no possibility of dialogue.

She turned slowly and began to retrace her steps. She passed the shut doors one by one.

'But at least I found it,' she thought. 'I found the room that doesn't get counted – or hardly ever.'

She wondered who else, before her, had found it.

'That depends on who does the counting,' Lockett had said.

So deep was she in her thoughts that she became lost. It had seemed simple enough coming the other way, but then she had been led by the whispers. The way back seemed twice as far.

Jessica had meant to go straight to the keys and return with as many as she could carry. She would find a basket to put them in then try them, one by one.

'Sooner or later I'll find the right one.'

She imagined the key turning in the lock, the great studded door swinging slowly open and then – what? That she could hardly imagine. That disembodied voice made flesh and blood. What would she be like, this sister of Harry, this imprisoned child? And how, simply by opening the door, would Jessica free her? That centuries-old child could not simply take her hand and go with her into the everyday world.

She entered the kitchen cautiously, meaning to make straight for the keys. But Mrs Lockett was there, up to the elbows in flour.

'Ah, there you are, dear. Have a nice game, did you?'

'Oh – yes, thanks.'

'Doing some baking.'

More cakes for Billy.

'Never knew children had such appetites!'

She was baking for one extra, a child who had not been counted.

'You're a good cook.'

Mrs Lockett smiled.

'Think I'll go out.' She had no choice. The keys were out of reach for the time being.

Jessica wandered across the courtyard, not really knowing where she would go. She half hoped that she would hear the scream of the peacock and that would decide the matter. But she heard only the usual daytime sounds of small birds.

She wondered whether Billy was still in Welshpool, raiding bins, swapping shrapnel. She guessed that he would be. He belonged on the streets, and those of Welshpool were the next best thing to those of London.

'But even when the war's over, where can he go? If his mother . . .?'

She stopped the thought. She did not want to think about mothers.

'Where are the deer? Keep watch, see how many I can count.'

She scanned about and behind her but saw no sign of them. When she gave up and looked ahead again she was almost level with the lake. She became aware of voices, familiar ones.

There they were, the three of them, by the lake. She ran towards them. Their backs were turned but she could see that they held rods, or sticks, and rings and ripples spread out, reflecting the sky in waves.

'Billy!'

They turned and looked at her, all three, with that hard, suspicious gaze.

'We're fishing for tiddlers,' Gilly told her. She raised her rod and a jam jar dangled from a string. 'Bovver! Try again!' She lowered it. 'Marlene's got a sock. Show 'er yer sock, Marlene!'

Marlene did no such thing, but Jessica saw that one of her legs was bare.

'We're going to fry 'em and eat 'em,' Billy told her. 'Pity we can't catch *them*!'

He pointed. Two swans floated at the far end of the lake.

'Roast goose! Yum yum!'

'Swan,' said Jessica.

'Them birds is pretty,' said Gilly, 'but I want to see that big blue 'un!'

She hauled up her jam jar and set off in the direction of the castle. The others went after her.

'I'm going to see that great big bird!'

'If there is one,' added Marlene sourly.

'An' we're to keep our eyes peeled for lions and tigers!'

At that the trio flicked their eyes nervously about. They saw no deer. Nor did they see that other figure pressed hard against the trunk of a tree, hiding.

'Ain't this *funny*!' said Gilly. 'All them trees! No 'ouses, no shops!'

'Did you warn them?' Jessica asked Billy.

He shrugged. She could have kicked him.

'About wishing!'

'Oh, *that*!'

'Know what I wish?' Gilly said. 'Wish I was back 'ome. Wish —'

'Don't!'

Gilly stared at her.

'Don't wish! Don't wish yourself away! Not while you're in Powis!'

'Why not?' demanded Marlene. 'Who're you bossing? My sister, not yours. Take no notice, Gilly.'

'Is that big bird reelly blue and green?'

'Yes,' said Jessica. 'But I don't think you'll see him.'

'Oh, la di dah! "Don't think you'll see him!"' Marlene mimicked. 'Too posh for vackys!'

'It's not that!'

'I shall see 'im, I shall!' Gilly wailed and clutched tightly at her sister's hand.

'Shut up and come on then,' Marlene told her, and marched on.

'What did you bring them for?' Jessica hissed to Billy.

'Keep yer hair on! Don't matter.'

They hurried after the other pair. The figure behind the tree watched them go.

'It's raining, it's pouring,
Hitler's hitting Goering!'

Gilly and Marlene were marching in unison, singing.

'Hurt 'is head and went to bed
And never got up in the morning!'

Billy was joining in. Jessica gave up.

They reached the castle and peered into the court-yard.

'Cor, ain't it big!'

'You reelly live there?'

'Who's that?'

Mrs Lockett emerged and started towards them. It was too late to run.

'Jessica?' She hurried her pace.

'Is it the queen?' Gilly whispered. 'Where's 'er crown?'

'Oh!' Mrs Lockett looked at the three of them with their grubby faces and unkempt hair. 'Who're these?'

'They're friends,' said Jessica swiftly. 'Stopping in Welshpool. They want to look at the gardens.'

'Oh.'

'An' that whopping bird!' said Gilly eagerly. Marlene gave her a dig.

'Is it all right, please? They won't do any harm.'

'Well ... I suppose ... You – are you the ones stopping with Megan – Mrs Jones?'

'Yes, they are,' said Jessica, before they could reply.

Mrs Lockett looked dubious.

'And what about him?' Billy, the one who had not been counted.

'Oh yes – they're all evacuees. So is it all right to go in the gardens?'

'Well – I suppose . . .'

'Oh, thank you! Come on!'

She tugged at Billy's arm and made for the winding path down to the gardens.

'Teatime soon, Jessica!' The voice came after them.

'Yes, Mrs Lockett, I shan't be late!'

'That weren't a queen!' said Gilly scornfully. 'Why's she living in a palace?'

'Castle,' Billy corrected.

'Look!' Gilly stopped dead and pointed. They were level with the leaden peacock.

'That's it!' said Billy. 'Like that!'

'You said a real bird. You said blue and green!'

''Tis real,' he told her. 'That's just a statcher! 'Tis real, ain't it?' He appealed to Jessica.

'Yes, it's real.' It was real, at any rate, in some world or other.

'Come on – show you where I sleep!'

They trailed along the terrace and mounted the stone steps. Broad daylight as it was, Jessica thought she felt a kind of shift and stir in the valley. It could never before have held so many children wishing themselves away.

'I'll have to warn them,' she thought. 'I'll have to.'

They peered into the orangery.

'Why've their heads been cut off?' Gilly pointed at the white busts.

'Lots of people 'ad their 'eads cut off in them days,' Billy said knowledgeably.

'I know!' Jessica moved past them and burrowed in the foliage. 'Your breakfast!' she said.

'Grub!'

'Ooh – biscuits!'

'They're mine!'

'You can all share it,' Jessica said. 'And I'll tell you a story. Sit down.'

They obeyed, eyes fixed on the food. Soon they were chewing and chomping, too busy to interrupt her.

Jessica began the story. She told first of Harry, the little lordling stolen away by the Green Lady. She told everything – the peacock, the running chain of stone-struck children, the child locked away in a high room. She told of the wishing, and the strange other Billy and Jessica already running free in the haunted valley.

Their jaws slackened. Their eyes grew round. They listened long after the food had vanished.

'And so you see,' she ended, 'we've got to save them.'

'Poor lickle fings!' sniffed Gilly dolefully.

'You should've seen 'em!' said Billy. 'All grey they was – 'orrible!'

'Was *they* vackys?' Marlene asked.

'Not exactly. But in a way, I suppose. But at least we'll go home when the war ends. They never will.'

'Unless we save 'em.'

'*We* play that game,' Marlene said. 'Chain Tag.'

'Fishes in a Net. Except this isn't exactly a game.'

'You're on!' Marlene dobbed Jessica and sprang to her feet. 'Come on!'

They fled, all three of them.

'No!' Jessica called after them. She did not want to play that game. Who knew what echoes it might stir? 'I'm not playing!'

They had disappeared. How could she ever catch them anyway? It was one thing to play the game in a confined space, in street or playground. Here there were acres where you could run and hide.

She walked slowly along the terrace towards the great crouching yews.

'Where are you?'

There was no reply.

'Billy?'

She stood and scanned about her. Her gaze travelled over the terraces, statues, yews.

'Marlene! Gilly!'

There was no reply. There was not the slightest movement. Then a peacock screamed.

Thirteen

A peacock screamed. Jessica shivered in the cool evening air.

Again!

He was there, waiting for her, fan unfurled. He seemed in no hurry to lead her. Tilt and turn, tilt and turn, neck stretched proudly at his own splendour.

'Pleased with himself!'

She shivered again. Those three had vanished earlier into the green depths of the garden, and then she had heard the peacock scream. Tonight, perhaps, there would be three more children on that stonestruck chain.

'What do you want?' she demanded. 'Where are the others?'

Gilly had longed to see him, the great big bird all blue and green. How her eyes must have stretched.

'Oooh,' Jessica could hear her saying, 'ain't you *bootiful*! Oh, I wish I lived here, I do!'

And as she said the words a part of her would have slid silently away, half-way to being stonestruck.

'And she doesn't want to live here – she wants to go home!'

She looked coldly at the preening bird and in that

moment his tail sank with a long, slow shudder. Then he stalked on.

He turned right at the bottom of the sloping path and Jessica knew at once where they were going. The low sun was behind the hill. The path was in shadow, dark and icy.

The pool lay thickly green and glassy. On the far bank moved that whitish mist. Slowly it thinned until she could see him, that fair sad boy. He reined in his horse and they gazed at one another from their separate worlds.

'Listen,' said Jessica in a fierce whisper, 'I will save you, I will!'

He smiled faintly.

'Where –' she scanned about her, 'where's *she*?'

'I think she's found another.'

'Child?'

He nodded.

Gilly, poor little Gilly with her runny nose and bright dreams of birds.

'Your sister!'

He waited.

'She sent me messages. I know where she is!'

'Beth!'

'I'm going to find the key, let her out!'

Slowly he shook his head.

'That's not the way.'

'What is, then, what *is*?'

She was desperate with the hopelessness of it all.

'If I know what to do, I'll do it! Tell me!'

'You must hold on. Hold on fast.'

'What do you *mean*?'

'Are you afraid?'

'Yes. No. I don't know.'

'Will you risk everything?'

She stared. She hardly knew what he was saying.

'Oh,' said a soft voice, 'no one dares risk everything.'

She was there, forming in the mist in streaks of green and gold.

'Did you think I was gone? Gone to ashes?'

'No.'

'Poor Priscilla!'

'*You* were Priscilla!'

That thin smile.

'Only a part of me. I play games. Children like games.'

'Not your kind! Not Fishes in a Net!'

'Ah. Perhaps you have no choice. Already you are half mine.'

'Don't listen!' said Harry.

She looked up at him and her face softened.

'It's a pity you won't speak to me. I only took the children for your sake.'

He turned away his head.

'He doesn't want them!' Jessica said. 'You catch them because you're cruel!'

'Not a word, not one single word. Oh, Harry, speak to me. If you'll speak to me I'll let them go, all of them!'

'Don't!' Jessica stepped forward. 'He doesn't want those children, you know he doesn't. There's only one person he wants.'

The Green Lady turned.

'His sister!'

'No! Never! It's *me* he shall love!'

'He hates you and loves his sister!'

'Go!' screamed the Green Lady then. 'Go!'

Jessica stood her ground but the mist came, and through it Harry's voice.

'Jessica, remember! Remember!'

Slowly the mist thinned. Gone. The whole valley was dim and hushed. It was a foreign land. Even the strong night smells of greenery were alien, and the last sunset twitters of birds. Jessica was filled with a huge, aching longing, a homesickness.

'What am I doing here?' she whispered. 'What am I doing here?'

She turned and saw that the peacock was there. He began to tread his way back along the darkening path. She heard the soft swish of his dragging tail. Her mind as she followed him was numb, blank. She did not even try to guess where he might be leading her.

On they went, and up, her eyes fixed on his gleaming back. Then he stopped. They were on the terrace where the seven arches were still faintly pink in the afterglow. She stood mystified. There were no whispers, no drumming feet. The leaden figures stared out over the silent valley. She went and stood by one of them, her hands on the cold stone of the balustrade. Looking down she saw that the stone had been pitted by time and weather until it was crusted like a barnacled wreck long under the sea. Silently, invisibly, time had worked its change, and all that time a stolen lordling had held his silence, waiting.

'For me!' she breathed. 'But why?'

She turned and saw that the peacock was still there and she knew that something would happen. His colours were muted in the dusk.

'Is it day or night?' she wondered. At what precise

moment did the light give way to darkness? What invisible line had to be crossed? At home in London she had never considered the matter. At home, as dusk fell, lights would be switched on and curtains drawn. Her mother would draw them carefully, checking for chinks.

'Put that light out!' The cry would echo in the deserted streets. Families huddled behind their black-out, praying that Jerry would not come tonight.

Here, she had stepped into another kind of danger. She did not know how to escape it. There was no shelter, no cellar.

'Oh,' she said aloud, 'I wish I was home! I wish –'

She stopped. Horrified, she clapped a hand to her mouth.

'Mind what you wish.'

It was too late.

'Jessica . . . Jessica . . . Jessica . . .'

There they were, the whispers. She turned to flee and saw that a single figure was running towards her out of the darkness. It sped noiselessly along the terrace then darted behind one of the arches. Already Jessica knew who it was. She knew before she saw the pale smudge of a face peering from behind a pillar.

Then came the sound of running feet, and voices. Her skin crawled at their badness, their spiteful chattering. She had brought them here by her own unguarded wishing.

She saw her other self cowering, terrified. The terrace was a dead end. There was no escape. She was trapped.

Now she could see the stonestruck children. Their eyes glittered in their grey faces, they grinned triumphantly.

'No!' she screamed, and ran wildly across their path and seized the hand of that other mirror self.

Afterwards, she could not remember how that hand felt, warm or cold. She could not remember the vanishing. She did not believe that her double had vanished into thin air, but had slid quietly and invisibly back into herself, become one with her again.

She faced her pursuers and they stopped dead. She was met by a battery of cold eyes.

'You can't touch me!' she said.

She was her own self, not a half-stonestruck shadow. Not one of them spoke. They stood eerily silent, not ordinary children at play, but children whose hearts had been turned to stone.

The chain broke. Each dropped its arm and lifted it to point a grey finger at herself. They stood in tableau and Jessica forced herself to hold their gaze. Her heart hammered so hard that it seemed they might hear it, might know her terror.

Those fingers pointed for what seemed an age. Then, as if at an unseen signal, their arms dropped. The hands joined. There was a chain again.

'The other one!' hissed the leader, and he turned and doubled back. The rest went after him pell-mell and she heard their hoarse whispers, 'After him! Catch him! Fish in a net!'

Away they streamed and dwindled into the dim distances of the night garden.

Jessica leaned against the cold brick of the archway and let out a long, shuddering breath. She tried to recall exactly what had just happened, but already she was not certain. She knew only that she had run across the very path of that stonestruck chain to save the other Jessica, that she had seized a hand that might have been warm, cold, or even half stone.

The peacock had gone. He had gone, perhaps, to lure some other child, the child now being pursued somewhere in the darkness.

'Oh, Billy!' she whispered.

It could be no one else.

'After him!' they had said.

She had saved herself, but could not save him. Slowly she started back along the terrace. Under the great brooding walls of the castle she went, and down the stone steps. She was level with the orangery when she heard, this time at a distance, a peacock scream. Then she ran.

On the lowest level she saw a figure ahead, plodding homeward. Lockett himself had been in the garden all the time.

'Lockett!' she gasped.

He turned.

'Jessica?'

'Did you hear?'

'Hear?'

'The children! The peacock!'

'I heard no peacock.'

'But you must've – just now!'

'I've heard no peacock since –' He broke off. 'It's not safe out here.'

All at once she knew.

'It was you!' She could hardly see his face in the dusk. 'That boy – the one who got away – came back!'

There was a long silence.

'It was me.'

Here at last was a true ally, one who had been before her into the dangerous places of the peacock.

'How old were you?'

'Ten. I was ten. There were seven of us at home. My father beat us.'

'And so you wished yourself away . . .'

'He'd take his belt from round his trousers, very slow, and smiling. Used to smile . . .'

'How awful!'

'I'd always loved this place, even then . . .'

'So you ran away here . . .'

'And wished I could stop for ever . . .'

'And saw the peacock . . .'

'I saw my other self . . .'

'And so you ran back home . . .'

He was shaking his head.

'I'd *meant* to join 'em.'

She could hardly take in his words.

'You mean . . .?'

'The stonestruck children. I went to join 'em.'

He had known what he was doing when he had run off to Powis. He had heard the stories all his life, been warned of the dangers.

'Thought it was a dream come true – to run free at Powis and be a child for ever.'

He had meant to disappear, like all those others.

'So why . . .?'

'I saw 'em. Have you?'

She nodded.

'Those terrible grey faces. Dream gone to nightmare, when I saw them.'

'So you ran back home.'

'Couldn't. Not straight off. Not and leave part of me

there. That was the worst part, night after night . . .'

That small boy had come back to Welshpool half crazed and babbling of peacocks. And no wonder. Night after night, alone, he had been pursued by those terrible children, taunted by their whispers.

'But you won, in the end!'

'Aye.' He drew a deep sigh.

'And I know how.'

'You have to go beyond the fear,' he said.

'Yes.'

'And when you do . . . the impossible happens.'

'Yes.'

They looked at one another, conspirators in the darkness, he for a moment her equal, a child again.

Fourteen

When Jessica woke she lay for a while remembering the previous day and at the same time tracing the pattern of sunlight on the ceiling.

'I'm me again,' she thought, and actually felt herself different, as if that shadow self had been draining part of her, leaving her empty.

She got up and peered at herself in the glass and half expected to see herself changed. She stared into her own eyes and smiled, feeling herself absolutely here and now, properly alive.

'I don't wish myself away,' she said aloud, and the words were a kind of charm.

Straight after breakfast she went to the orangery. Billy was not there.

'It doesn't necessarily mean he's been caught,' she told herself.

But yesterday she had heard the peacock scream, just after the three of them had disappeared into the garden.

'It could have been Marlene or Gilly.'

But neither of them was half-way to being stone-struck. Only Billy had a shadow self. She shivered, then tilted her head right back and saw the raw stone of the castle rearing skyward.

'Beth!' she called. 'I know your name now!'

There was no reply. She had not expected one. She was not even sure that the child could hear her. What timeless world did she inhabit, she, Harry and the stonestruck children?

'If they *are* set free, will they go back in their own time, or be here, now?'

She pictured that string of children marching towards 1940 Welshpool in their trews and boots, bonnets and petticoats.

'Another lot of evacuees!'

They would be gladly taken in, dressed in modern clothes, brought up as family. The good people of Welshpool guarded their secrets well. Those eerie children would not even be counted.

'It won't happen. Time doesn't work like that.'

How did time work? She did not know, but felt very strongly that it was more mysterious than she had ever guessed. Clocks and timetables only worked because people believed in them. Those messages that had fluttered down in the moonlight were signals of the hugeness, the mysteriousness of time.

'It won't be long now!' she called, and her voice certainly rang over the quiet gardens, but whether it travelled through time she could not tell.

Someone else heard it. A boy crouched, breath held, in the dusty heart of a yew. He had been there all night, had heard the cries of owls and peacocks, had seen a terrible thing. He felt that the world was coming to an end, and did not know how to stop it. He hardly even cared.

As Jessica passed through the iron gates she crossed her fingers and wished.

'Let him be there, let him be there!'

She shut out a picture of a stonestruck Billy, grey faced and cold-eyed, a sudden stranger.

In Welshpool something had changed. Jessica sensed it at once. There was an air of stir and secrets. Women stood in huddles, whispering. There was a curious absence of children – of Welsh children. There were none of the usual taunts, the endless choruses:

> 'Fleas, fleas
> Evacuees!'

The rude rowdy children of London were kings of the street. They yelled, ran, skipped and kicked balls along the gutters. One ran right to Jessica's feet and she stopped it neatly.

'Fanks!'

'Listen, do you know a boy called Billy?'

'Know lots!'

'Turnbull.'

'Yup!'

The boy dribbled the ball back towards the alley that was the goal. Jessica hurried after him.

'Have you seen him? Today?'

'Nope. *Goal!*'

A line of girls stood waiting as a long rope turned.

'A sailor went to sea sea sea . . .'

Jessica plucked the sleeve of the girl last in line.

'You seen Marlene and Gilly?'

'Nah.'

'Where're all the others? The ones who live here?'

The girl shrugged.

'Mas won't let 'em out.'

'Why?'

The girl shrugged again. Jessica thought she already knew the answer. Another child had disappeared. The old spell was still at work, even in a world of motorcars and telephones and wireless. The people of Welshpool were under a threat closer to home than the war.

Jessica hurried on, past the groups of women and their babbling Welsh, and ahead heard voices that were familiar, shrill and cockney.

> 'Cowardy cowardy custard
> Daren't eat mustard!'

They danced in glee, thumbed their noses, let out high-pitched cackles.

'You wait, mucky vackys!'

'You wait, mucky vackys,' they mocked. 'Whose ma won't let 'im out to play?'

The boy, goaded too far, ran out at them, fists raised, and the pair skipped back.

'Gareth! You come back here!' It was the boy's mother. 'You hear?' She cuffed his head as he dodged past her back into the house, and the girls redoubled their shrieks.

'And you get off, little devils! Go on – off with you!'

The door slammed.

'Marlene!'

The pair turned.

'Oh – lah di dah!' said Marlene, but Gilly ran to Jessica, face eager and lit.

'We seen 'im, we seen 'im, that great big bird! And his fevvers was blue! *Bootiful* 'e was!'

'Only an old bird,' said Marlene.

'But we never saw two of you and two of Billy,' Gilly said reproachfully.

'Now there will be two of you, as well,' Jessica thought.

The Green Lady's spell was gathering power.

'Where's Billy?'

Marlene shrugged.

'Dunno. Looked in 'is palace, 'ave you?'

'He's not there.'

'Finks 'e's clever. *We* might run off, might we, Gilly?'

'And go and live wiv that bird and –'

'No!' cried Jessica.

'Shall if we want!'

'But you – did you see a mist?'

'What?'

'A mist. Yesterday, when you saw the peacock.'

'What – a fog? Don't be daft. You're barmy. C'm'on, Gilly.' She marched off, dragging her sister after her.

'Don't go back there!'

For answer Marlene turned her head and stuck out her tongue.

Jessica combed Welshpool in vain for Billy.

'It doesn't necessarily mean he's not there, some- where,' she comforted herself. 'Could be hiding anywhere.'

He could be anywhere in the grounds of Powis, too, she thought, as she went back between the great stone gateposts. She walked slowly towards the castle and scanned left and right.

'But he's scared of deer,' she remembered, and had stopped looking when she glimpsed, to her right, a

sudden movement. She stopped and waited. There –
again – a head peering from behind a tree.

'Billy!' she shouted, and began to run. But the figure
turned and ran too, in the opposite direction. It ran
towards a dense wood that skirted the grounds, the
wood where she suspected the deer hid.

'Billy!' she screamed, but the figure ran on and was
swallowed among the trees.

Jessica halted, gasping for breath. What game was he
playing? Was it really Billy she had seen, or that strange
double? She was mystified.

'I'm coming back!' she shouted. 'After dinner!'

But by then the scent would have gone cold. By then
he could be anywhere.

As Jessica went along the stone passage to the kitchen
she could hear Mrs Lockett's voice.

'What? Last night? Oh, never!'

The telephone. A great cold wave swept over her.

'*Who?* Oh, what'll we do?'

More news. Terrible news.

'P'raps he hasn't . . . Could be hiding, couldn't he?'

He. Billy?

'But it's years since . . . oh dear oh dear. Listen . . .'
Mrs Lockett's voice sank almost to a whisper, 'Jessica,
she heard it, when she first came – *and* saw it, she says.
Oooh – what if *she* was to vanish!'

Now she knew for certain why the women of Welshpool were whispering in huddles, why only vackys
played in the streets.

'Now, Megan, we don't know, not for certain . . . you
know what they're like. Done it for devilment, I dare
say. Yes . . . no . . . I'll be over later, Megan.'

It was not a child of Welshpool that had disappeared.

It was a London child, a vacky.

The receiver was put down. Jessica went in.

'Oh, there you are!'

'Smells lovely,' Jessica said. She must act as if nothing was happening, as if she knew nothing whatever of that other world of the peacock.

'Had a nice morning, dear?' Mrs Lockett was acting, too.

'Went to Welshpool.'

'That's nice. Get some company. Not good for you, here in the gardens on your own.'

Not safe, she meant.

'See anyone you know, did you?'

'Oh yes. Marlene and Gilly.'

'Megan's little girls. You didn't . . . you don't know a boy called Trevor? Didn't see him, did you?'

So it was Trevor. Skinny little Trevor whom no one had wanted, and who had to sleep in the washhouse.

'I sort of know him. Didn't see him, though.'

'Well, if you do . . . you tell him to go home, will you?'

'Oh yes. Yes, I will.'

'Going into Welshpool this afternoon. Come with me, will you?'

Mrs Lockett did not want Jessica left alone in the dangerous gardens.

'Thought I'd stop in and read. Got some work to do before term starts.'

'Oh. Oh, that's all right, then.'

When Mrs Lockett had set off for Welshpool Jessica waited ten minutes, then went out. Somewhere out there were two boys, Billy and Trevor, and one at least of them was half-way to being stonestruck. She was not certain now which of them she had seen earlier, running in the park.

If Trevor had run off to Powis then surely he, too, must now be running with a double. If ever a child wished himself away it was he. She saw him as he had been at that last meeting, his precious letter snatched, the hopeless tears running down his face.

She did not really know where she was going or what she expected to happen. It was as if a tide were running, and she going with it. She went along the lower path, past the leaden peacock, and up the steps to the terraces. She had reached the second when she heard the peacock scream.

Fearfully she looked about. There he stood, at a little distance, pivoting, his great fan rocking.

Beyond him, towards the hunched yew hedge, was a mist, a particular patch of mist in the yellow sunlight.

The whispering began.

'Jessica . . . Jessica . . . Jessica . . .'

Slowly the mist thinned and she saw four figures. Billy, Trevor, Marlene, Gilly. They stood and looked back at her and gave no sign of recognition. These, she knew, were not real children, but ghosts of children, already part captives of the Green Lady. They watched her blankly, and she waited. It came, as she had known it would, the drumming of feet.

She turned and saw behind her a bank of mist, and through it glimpses of the stonestruck children.

'Run!' she screamed. 'Run!'

The others nodded and turned, all but one. Trevor stood undecided, as if bewildered.

'Run!' she screamed again, and as she did so Billy

ran back a few paces and seized Trevor's hand and pulled him after him.

Then Jessica felt the chill of mist as the chain of stonestruck children streamed past, and she put her hands over her ears to shut out the thunder of their feet and their spiteful hissing.

'They can't touch me, they can't touch me, they can't touch me.' She repeated the words over and over inside her head. She had reclaimed her ghost self, was safely here, now.

Very faint and echoing as if at the bottom of a deep well she heard the peacock scream. But when she took her hands from her ears and turned, he had gone. The gardens lay silent in the afternoon sun. It was impossible to imagine that out there, somewhere, four shadow children were being hunted.

Slowly her mind began to work again.

'Billy's safe!' Or as safe as he ever had been. Wherever he was he had not been caught like a fish in a net, was not stonestruck.

'Yooee! Vacky!'

She jumped. The voice was Billy's. There he was, that familiar ragtag figure, on the second terrace.

'You see that?'

'Course I did!' She ran towards him. He disappeared so often that even now she was not sure of him.

'They've got them others!'

'Not yet, they haven't! *Half* got them.'

'But where was you? Why wasn't you there?'

She told him. She told how she had run across the very path of the stonestruck chain to save her shadow self.

'Cor! Wasn't you scared?'

'Course! But listen, it worked!'

'Good job!' he said with feeling.

'That's the way to do it! Go beyond the fear.'

She was quoting Lockett's words.

'To what?'

'Not be frightened. Not run.'

'What – just stand there, and let 'em . . .' He shuddered.

'It works. I know it does. I did it before, remember, with Priscilla.'

'Might work for you!'

'No! For anyone! There's someone else –' She broke off. It was Lockett's secret.

'Who?'

'It doesn't matter. Years ago. Ages. And listen, *you* belong in this as much as I do.'

'How d'yer make that out? Don't even *live* 'ere – not proper.'

'But we met in London! And now you're here. Don't you see – you're meant to be!'

He looked at her, undecided.

'We've got to save them. Harry and his sister.'

'Never even seen this 'Arry. Nuffing to do wiv me.'

'I promised.'

'*I* didn't. Look, from London, we are. It's them Welsh kids they're after – and serve 'em right! I'm off!'

She ran after him.

'No! Just stay tonight!'

'No fear!'

'Please!'

'Nah fanks. I'm off to Welshpool and stop there!'

'In the castle!' The words were out before she had time to think them.

'*What?*' He stopped.

'It's enormous in there – no one'd know. And you'd be safe.'

His eyes travelled up the sheer stone walls.

'In a castle!'

'And then, when it's dark, we'll go out. And if once you see him – oh, Billy, he's so white and sad, and his sister . . .'

She blinked back the tears.

'Please, Billy, *please*!'

Fifteen

Mrs Lockett had gone to Welshpool. Lockett was away down below, digging for victory. It was easy to smuggle Billy into the castle.

'Cor – ain't it big?'

'This is only the bit where we live. You should see the rest.'

She found herself pleased to be entertaining a visitor so impressed.

'I know! I can show you the room where Beth is!'

'Who's she, when she's at 'ome?'

'The one who dropped the messages. His sister. Come on – there's plenty of time!'

She led him through the great high-ceilinged rooms with their draped furniture and bare walls.

'Cor!' he kept saying. 'Cor!'

'It's nothing to what it was before the war. All the best things have been packed away.'

'I might get a place like this when I'm rich.'

As they entered the warren of stone passages that led towards the locked room, Jessica stopped.

'Listen. That room – it isn't there – not for every-one.'

'You *what*? You're barmy, vacky!'

'I'm just telling you. It was there for me, and I think it'll be there for you.'

'I should blinking hope so!'

'You were there. You saw the messages. It's serious, Billy. You must . . . you must *want* it to be there.'

'You've got a screw loose.'

'At any rate, you believe it's there. Don't you?'

'Course. Saw them bits of paper, didn't I? Came from up 'ere somewhere.'

'All right. Come on. But you've got to be *serious*.'

Slowly she approached.

'Listen!'

That whisper, that single voice saying her name, half fearful, half questioning.

Billy licked his lips and looked over his shoulder.

She stopped outside the door. She tapped on it.

'It's me, Jessica!'

'And me, Billy!'

They waited.

'Here I write from this cold manor . . .'

Billy clutched at her arm.

'Have pity on me . . .'

The words were the same as before, spoken in that soft, hopeless voice.

'Long away from the world in this high room . . .'

'Say something!' Billy hissed.

Jessica shook her head. The record must play to its end.

'Save me, and save my brother . . .'

'We will!' Billy's patience was exhausted. He vainly pulled at the latch, hammered the door with his fists. 'You in there! It's us!'

He waited for a reply. None came. He kicked the door.

'She'd better look out, that's all! That green woman – she'd better look out!'

He kicked the door again. He was kicking the whole world.

'Bloomin' 'orrible lot! Shoving kids on trains, locking kids in rooms! We'll show 'em. We'll show 'em!'

He stepped back, breathless. In the silence came a child's voice, and this time it was not Jessica's name it spoke.

'Billy!' it whispered. 'Billy!'

He turned to Jessica.

'She said my name!' and he spoke proudly, as one who has been recognized and chosen.

'Of course,' she said, and knew now that he would stay, no matter what happened, and fight to the end.

They made their way back, every now and then peering from slits and windows for a sight of Mrs Lockett.

'You hungry?' she asked unnecessarily.

For answer he patted his stomach and rolled his eyes.

'Better get something now, before she gets back.'

In the kitchen rows of tarts stood cooling on racks. Billy darted past her and snatched one in each hand.

'Not too many,' she warned. 'Just a bit of everything.'

Already his cheeks were bulging, his chin covered in crumbs. He followed her into the larder, and boggled at the sight of hams, cheeses, butter, crusty bread and pies.

'Blimey!' he said thickly as Jessica swiftly cut slices of meat and bread.

He wandered about the kitchen, eating.

'Kitchen?' he said. 'More like blooming St Pancras station!'

Jessica giggled weakly. She opened the cupboard to reveal the rows of keys.

'An' blooming 'Olloway, 'n all!'

'It's a wonder you don't get stomach-ache,' she told him.

'World's fastest eater!' he boasted. It seemed possible.

'You'd better come to my room,' she said.

He entered, incongruous in his grubby rags. He stared at the row of books, the neatly made bed, the chest of drawers with its mirror and lace mats.

'There's only one bed!'

'Course!'

'You mean it's yours – all yours?'

She had a sudden picture of the London streets with their terraces of narrow houses, two up, two down.

'Lucky, aren't I?'

He threw himself on the bed and the plump eiderdown and let out a groan of pure pleasure. He rolled and curled and pressed his limbs, his face into the softness.

'Any minute now he'll start purring,' she thought.

'Oooh,' he moaned. 'Luverly, luverly . . .'

It seemed that he might never get up. She waited. In the end he did sit up. His eyes went to the photograph.

'That your ma and pa?'

'Yes.' She hesitated. 'But, Billy. . .' She suddenly wanted to put it into words, the terrible secret she was carrying.

'Something terrible's happened to one of them . . .'

He at least would understand. He had lost his own family in that smoking rubble.

'But I don't know which! I heard her talking on the

phone – she hasn't said anything – it could be either of them.'

To her horror she felt tears slide down her cheeks. Hastily she brushed them away.

'Don't cry, vacky,' he said gruffly. 'No use bawling, yer know.'

'I know. I know.'

'Worse things 'appen at sea.' He mechanically repeated the silly, pointless words he had heard the grown-ups say.

'I know,' she half sobbed, and brushed her eyes again.

'No use crying over spilt milk.' Another formula, another piece of grown-up wisdom.

'Oh, Billy, I do . . .' he looked at her, '*like* you!'

He grinned then, hugely, sitting cross-legged with careless boots on the crumpled eiderdown.

'Yer not bad yerself, vacky!'

She took her journal from the drawer.

'Look!'

'What is it?'

'The story. I'm writing it all down. About the peacock and the Green Lady.'

'Cor! Ain't yer clever, lah di dah!'

'I must write it down before we go out tonight.'

'What – case we never come back?'

'Don't say that!'

'I ain't scared. Hey – she said my name!'

There were few, these days, who said Billy's name.

'I'll do it now.'

'Fink I'll 'ave a kip . . . ooh, luverly grub . . .' He flopped back and shut his eyes and smiled a beatific smile.

'She won't come in.' Jessica found her pen and prepared to write. 'Only in the mornings to tidy up, and last thing at night.'

There was no answer but for a loud snore. Snore, whistle . . . snore, whistle . . . It was evidently one of his party tricks.

'You might as well *really* go to sleep,' she told him. 'You won't get much tonight.'

The evening seemed endless. Now that Billy was in Jessica's room it was too risky to smuggle him out and then in again. She found a pack of cards and they played snap and gin rummy, talking in whispers, smothering their giggles.

As dusk fell Jessica said, 'Under the bed now.'

Billy grimaced. He had fallen in love with the soft bed and its plump eiderdown, would have spent the rest of his life on it, it seemed.

'I'll bring you some biscuits.'

She went to the kitchen, and sat at the table while Mrs Lockett warmed up the milk for Ovaltine. Not a word had been said at teatime about the missing boy. Not a word was said now.

'I'm tired. I'll take it to my room, can I?'

She shared the drink and biscuits with Billy.

'Under the bed now,' she said again.

'What about this?' He opened the wardrobe and peered in.

'Too risky. What if the door swung open?'

They snorted at the picture of Mrs Lockett coming in to say goodnight to her tame, clean visitor and finding a mucky vacky in the wardrobe. Billy rolled under the bed. Jessica drew the curtains.

'Air raid shelter!' came his muffled voice.

'Wait for the all-clear!'

Jessica had got into bed fully dressed but for her shoes, and kept the covers right up to her chin. There was not long to wait before Mrs Lockett made her nightly visit. She leaned stiffly over and planted a dry kiss on Jessica's forehead.

'Goodnight then, dear.'

'Night, Mrs Lockett.' Jessica made her voice drowsy.

'Sweet dreams.' She said it mechanically, as she always did. The door closed behind her.

They waited until they heard the Locketts going past to their own room, and then for half an hour after that. The time had come.

They crossed the courtyard and as they came out into the gardens felt the night fathomless about them. Jessica silently summoned the peacock, willed him there. She caught Billy's sleeve.

'And remember,' she whispered, 'mind what you wish!'

The peacock screamed. He was suddenly there, a gleaming shape, and at once turned and began to lead them along the sour damp path that led to the pool. He had come tonight at Jessica's own bidding. It was as if he were a puppet and she pulling the strings. They went in silence, the only sound the scuff of their footsteps and now and then the hooting of an owl.

When they emerged by the pool it was silver under the moonlight, smooth as glass. Jessica looked over to the other side, and there he was, on his white horse, trappings glinting.

'That 'im?' Billy whispered.

She nodded. Slowly he came, his fair head bowed and shining whitely. They waited, and at last he halted by them. They stared up at his sad pale face.

'Jessica,' he said.

'Yes. And I've brought Billy. He's going to help me.'

The boy's gaze travelled to Billy's upturned face. He shook his head.

'She'll never let me go.'

'We'll make her!'

'She says she has another fish to catch.'

Jessica's heart jumped. Trevor! Was he out there somewhere in the darkness at this very moment, running for his very life?

'She won't catch me!' said Billy fiercely.

The boy did not reply, and then they noticed the tears running down his pallid cheeks. He twitched the reins and the horse moved on.

'We'll save you!' Jessica cried.

'We will, we bloomin' will!'

He seemed not to hear. Already he was melting into the dark.

'He doesn't believe us!'

'Come on – Trevor!'

They raced back and under the terraces, then up. At the top they paused for breath.

'We – don't know – where 'e is!' Billy gasped.

'If only I'd warned him! Oh, poor Trevor!'

She could only guess at his terror, alone out there in the darkness.

'Trevor!' Billy shouted. 'Trevor!'

The words rang over the deserted garden.

'Where shall we *look*? We got to look!'

Jessica did not know.

'You will not find him now,' said a soft voice.

They whirled about. The Green Lady, silvered with moonlight, stood watching them. As they stared, somewhere in the distance a peacock screamed. She smiled.

'There!' She was triumphant. 'Another fish!'

'Oh, Trevor!'

'It was easy. I spoke to him gently, as a mother would.'

She moved her gaze to Billy.

'You . . .' she murmured. 'Already half mine, by your own wishing.'

'I never meant it!'

'Too late,' she said.

'It's not!' cried Jessica. 'Don't listen, Billy!'

Now the Green Lady was looking at her.

'Do you not want to save your friends? All three of them?'

'Yes, and I will!'

'It is easy, so easy. Come with me now, and I will set them free.'

Again the peacock screamed.

'It is you Harry has been waiting for.'

'Yes – to save him!'

'He wants only you. Come with me . . . think . . . to be a child for ever . . .' Her voice was tender, coaxing.

Gazing into those silvered eyes Jessica could almost believe her, could feel the pull of the spellbound valley, and half wish to be drowned in it.

'Come, Jessica, come . . .' She stretched out a hand.

Still held by her gaze, Jessica started to stretch out her own hand to take it.

'It's a trick!' Billy grabbed her hand and pulled it back.

'You get off – get off!' He stood at bay, glaring his defiance.

Her face went thin and cold.

'You!' she spat. 'You next!'

And then she was shimmering, pulled into threads, a streak of silver and green, then gone.

'Oh, Billy!' Jessica whispered. 'Now what?'

'Don't care! She's not getting me!'

'She's got Trevor.'

'Look!' He pointed.

The peacock was there. He stood motionless, a sign that they not safe yet, that they still stood on the edge of their world and his. This time he had not come at Jessica's bidding. He had his own power.

Then they knew why. Faintly, far away, they heard the footsteps of the stonestruck children.

'They're coming!' Billy clutched at Jessica's hand more tightly than ever. 'Come on!'

He made to run, back down the steps and along the path to safety.

'No – look!'

Already they were in sight, and ahead of them a small figure flying.

''S me!' Billy tried to tug his hand free. Now it was she who was holding him back.

'No! It's too late! Do what I did!'

Already the shadow Billy had almost reached them and the chain was right at his heels.

'*Do* it!' Jessica screamed, and loosing her hold gave Billy a push.

He staggered forward, then put out his hand to catch that of the fugitive.

This time Jessica actually saw it happen. She saw the

two Billys merge and slide together, become one.

Then the stonestruck children were there. As before, they stopped, panting. Jessica stepped forward to stand by Billy.

'You can't touch us!'

Then, as before, the chain broke. Each child raised an arm and pointed a finger. She forced herself to look at those dead, unsmiling faces and saw, with horror, the one she was looking for.

She hardly recognized him, grey-faced and glittering-eyed as the rest. His finger, too, pointed inexorably.

'Trevor!'

He made no sign. He was not there. The child he had been was in the thrall of the Green Lady. He was stonestruck.

'Trevor!' she heard Billy whisper.

Slowly the pointed fingers dropped. The chain formed again. Trevor was the last, linking his hand with another as if he had played the game for centuries.

'No!' yelled Billy.

It was useless. The grey face was impassive. He was beyond their reach now.

Jessica watched desperately as the leader set off at a run and the rest followed, gathering momentum. They turned in an arc and wheeled back the way they had come and dwindled into the darkness.

'Oh, Trevor!' She felt tears hot on her cheek. 'He was so little and scared!'

'Told you, vacky – no use bawling.'

'It's my fault!' she sobbed. 'It's all my fault!'

Sixteen

Jessica stirred, flung out an arm and felt warm flesh. Then she remembered. She turned her head and saw that Billy was still sleeping. His face looked different, younger. She raised herself on an elbow and stared down at it, as she had gazed at her own reflection yesterday. Had his features softened because he was asleep, or because he had reclaimed his shadow self, was no longer half-way to being stonestruck? She could not tell.

Then she remembered Trevor. His pale, frightened face was now set hard and grey, his pleading eyes were turned to pebbles. Stonestruck.

Gently she shook Billy's shoulder. He muttered and twitched and threw out an arm.

'Billy! Billy!'

He opened his eyes.

'Where? What? Oh!'

He sat bolt upright.

'We must go! Look at the time! He'll be there already!'

She swung her legs over the side of the bed. She, too, had slept in her clothes.

'Soon be as smelly as the rest of them!' she thought.

They tiptoed along the passage and out into the courtyard. Once there, they ran towards the gardens, the glittering valley.

'Today!' shouted Jessica. 'We'll do it today!'

Now, in the clear morning, it all seemed possible.

'We'll do it! We'll show 'em!'

Billy believed it, too.

Lockett, as she had guessed, was already at work. At their approach he straightened and leaned on his spade.

'Lockett!'

'So you've heard,' he said.

'Yes! And we're going to rescue him! This is Billy.'

'Mornin', mister!'

'He's my friend. And listen.'

She told him everything.

'And we did it – we both did it – same as you!' she finished. 'When Billy did it, I *saw* it, I saw –'

'*I* didn't,' put in Billy. 'Dead creepy it was.'

'But what now?' she asked. 'How do we save *them*?'

He did not answer at first. He seemed to be thinking.

'Same way, I reckon,' he said at last.

'But how *can* we? There's only two of us!'

'It's something I've thought of, on and off, over the years,' he said. 'Every time there's another child stone-struck, her power grows.'

'And she caught another last night!'

'We've been too long afraid of her in Welshpool.' He seemed almost to be talking to himself.

'And afraid to count children,' Jessica said. 'Never count children twice – ever.'

'That's it,' he agreed.

'That's why they don't even know Billy's missing!'

'Invisible vacky!' said Billy.

'I've often thought – if all the Welshpool children was to march in here, they could – turn the tables.'

'But they never would! Yesterday they were all indoors!'

'Oh yes,' agreed Lockett. 'They would be.'

'*Vackys* wasn't,' said Billy.

The children of London had run stamping through the streets. They had yelled, chased, sung. And it was a child from London who had been stolen.

'That's it!' Jessica cried. 'That's *it*!'

They both looked at her.

'*They're* not scared! And when they hear about Trevor, they'll be mad! No wonder he ran off – oh, Lockett, she made him sleep in the washhouse!'

'Old witch,' said Billy. 'They're all stopping with witches.'

'There's more vackys than there are in that chain! If *we* made a chain –'

'It'd *do* 'em!' Billy yelled. 'Not them catch us – us catch them!'

'Yes!'

Safety in numbers – it was true. She knew how fearless she would be in a string of London vackys, hand in hand. And fearlessness, it seemed, was the name of the game.

'Beat 'em at their own game!' Lockett was beginning to smile. 'I've dreamed of that!'

'It'd work! I know it would!'

'Aye. I believe it would. But how?'

'Me! I'll make 'em!' Billy was alight!'

'Know 'em, do you?'

'They all know me – Billy Turnbull!'

'Children from London . . .' Lockett murmured. 'That'd be a strange thing . . .'

'It has to be!' Jessica told him. 'The others wouldn't dare. And their mothers wouldn't let them.'

'I'll round 'em up!'

'Lockett . . . if we do it . . . will it set Harry free as well, and his sister?'

'Oh yes. It's all of a piece.'

'We'll do it!'

'And her gone for ever. She'll fight, mind. But there's only one thing to remember.'

'I know.'

'The world's full of fear. It's fear she feeds on.'

'I know.'

'Could wish *I'd* been braver . . .'

'You *were*! You escaped, remember!'

'And now it's children from London'll break the spell.'

'Vackys!' said Billy. 'We'll show 'em! I'll go now!'

'No! It's too early! They won't even be up.'

He grimaced.

'Get some grub, then. Go round the bins.'

Jessica looked at Lockett.

'Billy's been living rough.'

'Don't stop anywhere,' he boasted.

'He wasn't counted, you see.'

'Living out the bins, is it? Then I reckon you'd better come with me now and get a proper breakfast.'

'Lockett! Lockett!' They all turned. It was Mrs Lockett, red and excited-looking. 'Oh – Jessica, you're there! Been looking everywhere!'

'What?'

'Your mother – on the telephone!'

'What? *What?*'

'It's all right! He's safe!'

'Dad!'

'Thought he was missing, see, presumed . . . But he's safe, she says!'

Jessica felt a huge lightness, the lifting of a weight. The world was safe again.

'For me, at any rate,' she thought. 'And soon for all of us!'

Now Mrs Lockett was looking at Billy.

'Him again,' she said. 'Why's he here?'

'Long story, Rhoda,' Lockett said. 'Plenty to tell. Breakfast first.'

Mrs Lockett produced a breakfast for Billy – one such as he had never seen before, judging by his face when he saw it, and his wolfish eating.

Lockett told her the plan. She was aghast.

'Never!' she cried. 'What if they was *all* to disappear!'

'It's the only way to get the boy back, Rhoda. Might never've been counted, but he's got a mam and dad'll want him back.'

'You're not to go, Jessica! Responsible for you, I am!'

'And me,' Lockett reminded her. 'She must go, and lead the chain.'

'Oh, I don't know, I don't know!'

'It'd better be tonight,' Lockett said. 'Sunset.'

The sky was streaked red and yellow by the setting sun. Jessica and Billy pounded through the park towards Welshpool. Deer scattered before them, dew flashed up from their heels.

'I'm Billy the Conqueror. 'Ere I come!'

174

A war was to be fought, and it was not hundreds of miles away, fought by faceless soldiers in unimaginable places. This was one for them, one they could fight and win. Jessica tilted forwards on the balls of her feet and felt she might actually take off and fly.

Welshpool was as it had been yesterday. People stood in huddles, talking in low voices. After fifty years the old terror had reawakened.

But the children from London had taken possession of the twilit streets. They rolled marbles in the gutters and raced and hopscotched and the air was filled with their screams and laughter. They did not understand why, but all at once they were free and left to their own devices.

'One potater two potater three potater four!'

A huddle of boys with their fists stuck out were being counted out for a game. Billy raced to them, pushed his way in.

'Gerroff!'

'I got a game! I got a real game!'

Jessica knew that she could not imitate him. He was one of them, she an outsider. If she was to spread the word she must first find Marlene and Gilly.

'In and out the windows,
In and out the windows . . .'

She scanned the group of girls. Not there. Up and down Broad Street and High Street she went, and down the little alleys, Bear Passage, Hopkins Passage, Daxe's Row. In the end it was they who found her, ran into her full tilt.

''Elp!' yelled Marlene and dropped her apple and

went after it. Gilly stood and bit into her own. Marlene wiped hers on her sleeve and followed suit. The pair stood looking at her, biting and chomping.

'Thank goodness I've found you!'

'Why?' demanded Marlene.

'We need you – Billy and me!'

'That Billy Turnbull's a blooming liar!'

'Said there was *two* of 'im, and *we* never seen 'em!'

'There aren't any more,' Jessica said. 'But there are two of you!'

'Yer what?'

'I've seen them. You saw the peacock!'

'Ooh, bootiful 'e was!' sighed Gilly through her apple.

'And now she's got Trevor! The Green Lady!'

''E's run off. *I* might, and all.'

'He hasn't! At least, he did to start with, but now . . .'

They looked at her, calmly chewing.

'He's stonestruck!'

Gilly, at least, seemed interested.

'What, yer mean in that gang plays Chain Tag?'

'Yes.'

'And will 'e stop for ever and ever?'

'Yes – unless – oh, you've got to help!'

'And has 'is face gone grey?'

'Yes!'

'Blimey!' remarked Marlene, impressed at last. 'Bet 'e looks 'orrible!'

'He lives on our street,' Gilly said. 'What'll 'is ma say?'

'She'll never see him again,' Jessica said. 'Not unless you help.'

Now, at last, they understood.

'Go on then – we'll 'elp! We'll show them Welshpool kids!'

Quickly Jessica told them the plan.

'And would *we* see them kids wiv grey faces?' Gilly was round-eyed, awestruck.

'But there's no need to be frightened. There's more of us than them.'

'And we can run faster!' said Marlene. 'Fastest runner in our street, I am! Come on! All the vackys! Whoopee!'

'Three cheers for the vackys!' shouted Gilly, going after her. ''Ip 'ip 'ooray, 'ip 'ip 'ooray!'

Jessica went after them. Back on Broad Street she could see that Billy had done his work well. A string of children, hands held, was tearing towards her.

'Fishes in a net, fishes in a net!' they chanted.

The people of Welshpool watched, helpless. The world had gone mad. Those evacuees had been taunted and jeered at. Now, they were sweeping through the town like conquerors. Joined as they were hand in hand, they were a living force, unstoppable.

All the time the chain was growing as the London children saw what was afoot and joined in with glee. Half of them did not know why. They knew only that it felt good to be running hands held and with the courage of numbers.

Billy was leading the chain, and Jessica ran to seize his free hand and herself become the leader.

'You did it!'

'We'll show 'em! Vackys to the rescue!'

'Vackys to the rescue!' The cry went up along the chain.

''Ere, let us in!' Billy let go of the hand of the boy

behind him and let Marlene and Gilly in. Now they were ready, all the uncounted children from London, to do battle.

Jessica led the chain from Broad Street into the lane that led to the park.

'Oh – whatever?'

'What'll become of them!'

'Oh, stop! Stop!'

The people of Welshpool were hurrying after them, aghast. Jessica led the chain through the gates, then stopped. All along the line they halted, breathless.

'Walk now! Keep hands joined, but walk! We've got to save our breath for the real game!'

'Save Trevor!'

'Save Trevor!' they yelled in response.

'Vackys for ever!'

'Vackys for ever!'

Jessica saw that the people of Welshpool had stopped at the gates. They were held there by a lifetime of superstition and terror. She turned and looked ahead at the darkening meadows, at the great dense banks of trees and turreted outline of the castle. Then she began to march.

'Daisy, Daisy, give me your answer do!' Billy struck up the song behind her.

'I'm half crazy, all for the love of you!' A chorus of children's voices joined in.

Through the gleaming buttercup meadow they marched, then under the massive walls of the castle itself.

> 'It's a long way to Tipperary,
> It's a long way to go . . .'

Now they were passing the entrance to the courtyard. Looking to her left, Jessica saw the figures of the Locketts. With her free hand she waved, and saw Lockett's arm rise in answer.

Down towards the gardens she went, and now the singing was softer, as if instinctively the children knew that they were treading perilous ground.

As Jessica drew level with the orangery and halted, the singing died away altogether, in mid song. The silence was enormous. Jessica turned, and saw the string of pale faces stretching away behind her in the gloom.

'Remember – whatever you see, whatever happens – don't be afraid!'

'And keep 'olding 'ands!' It was Billy, playing sergeant-major, going into battle. 'If yer don't, we're done for!'

Silence. Then, tearing that silence, the scream of a peacock. A stir ran down the line.

'It's that big bird!' Gilly whispered.

The peacock appeared. He made himself out of air. His great fan was unfurled and he dipped and swayed. Whispers hissed down the line.

'Cor!'

'Look at that!'

The peacock turned and trod away. Jessica followed. He was making for the tunnel of yew that led to the lower gardens. They went in silence, almost tiptoe in this strange game of follow-my-leader. Under the yew they went, in the drily scented darkness and down the steps beyond.

Then they were on the wide grassy stretch with the wilderness beyond. Never before had the peacock stalked so far and Jessica, eyes fixed on the shadowy thickets beyond, wondered if this were some kind of trap.

The peacock halted. Straining her eyes into the dusk, Jessica made out two figures running out of the trees. They came flying full tilt, legs gleaming.

'It's us!' came Marlene's fearful whisper. 'Oooh, it's us!'

At their heels came the chain of stonestruck children. They came thundering and chanting.

'Fishes in a net, fishes in a net!'

'Get 'em! Get 'em!'

The hands of the vackys squeezed tight.

'Look – it's Marlene!'

'And Gilly!'

Jessica moved then. She ran to meet the running girls and the chain came after her, she could feel its power through Billy's fingers. Now the shadow selves were between two chains. Terrified they halted, looking wildly about them.

'Marlene! Here – it's us!'

By now the stonestruck children were almost upon them, but the girls began to run again, hand in hand, towards the other chain. They came flying. Jessica turned.

'Marlene! Gilly! Quick!'

Marlene and Gilly hesitated only for an instant. Then they loosed hands and each stretched out to her double, and they each became one again. It happened in the twinkling of an eye.

'Cor!' came Billy's whisper. 'It's a blooming miracle!' and a gust of whispers went down the line.

The stonestruck children, cheated of their quarry, halted. Jessica's heart beat hard. This was the moment of truth. When the London children saw those terrible grey faces, those glittering eyes, would their nerve hold? There was silence but for their panting breath. The two lines of children faced one another, waiting for the first move.

It was Billy who made it.

'After 'em! Vackys to the rescue!'

At that the stonestruck children let out piercing, savage screams and the leader, his face twisted, turned and the whole chain went after him. As they wheeled, Jessica glimpsed Trevor's stony face. He was last in line, and it was his hand she must catch.

The chase was on. They tore through the twilit gardens, twisting and turning. After a time the cries and yells died away. They ran in silence, intent and desperate.

Now they were streaming under the arch of yew, now on the terrace past the orangery, and Jessica's fingers strained ahead for the touch of a stone hand. She could see it now, only inches away.

Now . . . now . . .

'Ah.' Her fingers closed on that grey hand.

And then it was as if time stood still. Everything stopped. They froze, those two chains, in mid flight, knees still bent, feet poised in mid air.

In the void a scream rang out, and it was not the scream of a peacock. The Green Lady was there, screaming, screaming. A pillar of emerald flame sprang up about her, and the great spearing flames shot skyward above her head. She writhed and clawed with her long white fingers, but she was imprisoned in fire. Her screams were soundless now, drowned in the roar. Clothed in fire she shimmered and shrivelled and at last was gone. The tall flames died until they were little licking tongues, then flickered out.

A huge, whispering sigh went through the valley, and with it came light, easing out of the darkness. A bright incredible dawn came, and in it the frozen limbs of the children stirred and came to life again. They were released.

In the golden light Jessica saw that the stonestruck children were live and rosy. Some had dark hair, some fair. They were blue- or brown-eyed and were like any other children, anywhere. They dropped hands, stretched, stared, laughed.

'Cor!' came Billy's whisper again. 'It's a bloomin' miracle!'

Trevor stood blinking, owl-like, as if awoken from a bad dream.

'Look!' Jessica pointed.

They followed her finger. There, in the meadow below, was a white horse with a boy riding. And towards him went the running figure of a girl, jewel bright in the sunlight. They heard her voice.

'Harry! Harry!'

'Beth!'

He reined in his horse, and as his sister reached him, leaned to pull her up. She sat before him in the saddle, and both looked upward and raised a hand in salute. Then they rode on.

'Home!' cried one of the released children, and she began to run, blue skirts lifting.

'Home! Home!' the cry went up.

Those other children scattered and ran, making for homes they had left years ago – centuries.

'Home! Home!'

The dazed children from London watched as each went, and each as it ran suddenly vanished, snuffed out like a candle flame. All about them the air was punctured with little vanishings – pft pft pft!

The last one disappeared. The light faded. It went in a long silent wave and with it the colour drained from stone, flower, tree. It was night again.

'Trevor!' Jessica was seized with sudden panic, but she saw him there, and snatched his hand. He looked at her as one sleep-walking.

'I saw . . . I saw a peacock . . . I saw –'

The peacock! There was no sign of him. He, too, had vanished. He had played his part in the story, and gone.

'Yippee!' came Billy's exultant shout. 'We done it! We done it! Vackys from London – form a line in twos!'

They shuffled into line, two by two. Jessica and Trevor led, Gilly and Marlene behind them. Billy stood at the head, sergeant-major.

'Atten – shun!'

Obediently they straightened up and clicked their heels.

'Vackys from London – about turn!'

Each spun about.

'Quick – march! Left, right, left, right!'

He led the way and the rest followed, chanting in unison, 'Left, right, left, right!'

Tonight they had played a game such as they had never played before. They had fought a battle and won. Back under the walls of the castle they wound, and off again across the darkened meadows, singing now.

'It's a long way to Tipperary,
It's a long way to go!'

That strange ragged army went marching through the cold dewfall. They reached the iron gates to Welshpool and the whole town was there to greet them, children and all. A cry went up as the leaders marched through, and one of them was the boy feared missing, stonestruck.

'There he is!'

'That's him!'

'We done it!' Billy yelled. 'We got 'im back! We got 'em all back!'

'Three cheers for the vackys!' came a voice from the crowd.

'Hip hip hoorah! Hip hip hoorah! Hip hip hoorah!'

The great roar died away. The vackys were grinning now, and proud. They had done a hard thing. The last of them passed through the gate of Powis.

'Vackys – halt!' yelled Billy.

They stamped to a halt. Then Jessica sprang forward.

'Vackys from London – number from the left! Trevor!'

'One!' piped Trevor.

'Two!' Marlene.

'Free!' Gilly.

Jessica looked at Billy as the numbering voices went down the line. Their eyes met as they had that first time, over the smouldering rubble in a London street. She did not speak, but knew that her message was plain. Their eyes were locked for what seemed an age. Then, suddenly, he nodded and grinned, a huge wide grin. He leapt forward and joined the line, as a girl was calling, 'Twenty-two!'

'Twenty-*free*!' he yelled.

Billy was back in the world again, counted.